C.B. DEMILLE:
THE MAN WHO INVENTED HOLLYWOOD

A Novel
By
Robert Hammond

New Way
PRESS
www.newwaypress.com

The following work combines parody, satire, historical fiction, creative nonfiction, apocryphal accounts, allegory, parable, fable, urban legend, mythology, poetic license, scholarly research, fair use, works in the public domain, and the author's fertile imagination. Although inspired by the real life and work of the visionary director Cecil B. DeMille, certain situations, characterizations, and conversations were created for literary entertainment and educational purposes.

Published in the United States
by New Way Press.
www.newwaypress.com

Library of Congress Control Number: 2012915293

ISBN- 13: 978-0615680552
ISBN- 10:0615680550

C. B. DeMille

For Lesa

"Most of us serve our ideals by fits and starts. The person who makes a success of living is the one who sees his goal steadily and aims for it unswervingly. That is dedication."

~ Cecil B. DeMille

C.B. DEMILLE:
THE MAN WHO INVENTED HOLLYWOOD

HOLLYWOOD 1880's

Everybody knows that Cecil B. DeMille was the most powerful moviemaker Hollywood has ever known. In fact, he invented Hollywood.

Before DeMille made his fateful trip from New York in 1913, Southern California was nothing more than orange groves and desert, with a few scattered ranches and barns and dirt roads. What you might not know is that a prohibitionist real estate developer named Horace Wilcox and his wife, Daeida founded Hollywood in the late 1880's. Horace was a religious man who wanted to form a community of like-minded, clean living folks free from the corruption of alcohol and jazz music. Little did they know how things would eventually turn out.

PROLOGUE

And God said,
"Let there be light."
And there was light.
And from this light,
God created life upon earth.

OLD THEATER

A red butterfly fluttered into the window of a dark and empty theater, touching down only for a holy instant upon the empty stage, then off again, up and out the window vanishing into the sun.

Inside the theater, the faded curtains hung loosely, worn by time and inattention as an unseen man's voice shouted, "Action!" The single word echoed, multiplying through the lonely timbers, resonating in the air, and then fading into nothingness.

Nothing happened. A long silence begged for interruption.

"I said action!" The man's voice grew louder, stronger, echoing once again across the empty stage.

"Where the hell is everyone?" His voice betrayed a desperate tone.

A shaft of sunlight angled in through the window, revealing the signature custom boots of aging, balding Cecil B. DeMille. He wore jodhpurs and carried a large megaphone.

He rose from his director's chair. "Where are my extras?" he yelled.

Nothing but an empty stage.

Slowly, a hand drew back the stage curtain...

CHAPTER 1

C.B. DeMille sat in his director's chair, lowering the megaphone from his mouth. Desert winds swept sparkling desert sands against steep cliffs. The saffron sun scattered light and shadows across the shimmering dunes, revealing the Sphinx rising in the distance, and rows and rows of pyramids.

DeMille's forty-year-old daughter Ciddy, naturally pretty, her kind eyes shimmering with the natural wonder and imagination of a young girl, sat next to him. DeMille handed Ciddy his wooden cane, worn by time and use.

He turned to her slowly and asked, "Can you keep an eye on this?"

Ciddy took the cane in her hands and looked at it fondly then looking up at her father. "Oh, you think you don't need it anymore?" she asked.

"Something like that," he said with a twinkle in his eyes.

A young camera assistant kneeled before the camera and clapped the slate. "The Ten Commandments. Scene 70."

DeMille raised the megaphone back to his mouth. "Action!" he shouted.

Hundreds of horses and chariots galloped along the edge of the cliffs edging down the steep incline. Three cameramen caught the action from different angles.

The chariots descended to the bottom of the steep dunes in clouds of dust.

CHAPTER 2

NEW YORK, 1913

The small Manhattan apartment was neatly furnished. Constance DeMille laid out the modest silver service on the dinner table. Her dark hair was pinned back in a bun; her dark eyes gave her a Latin appearance. Five-year-old daughter Ciddy, cute and precocious, pouted while standing on the sofa, looking out the window.

Cecil B. DeMille was struggling as a theater producer, having attained sporadic success as an actor and playwright. Constance had been a stage actress. They met on the stage and were married within a year. They spent their wedding night in the Ritz-Carlton Hotel. Constance cautioned Cecil to be careful with all the nice furniture. He responded by dancing on the dining room table. From that night on, she never told him what to do again.

Ciddy, whose birth name was Cecilia, was the couple's only natural born child. After she was born, the doctor confirmed that Constance would never be able to have children again.

"When is father coming home? I want father! I want father!" Ciddy demanded as she turned to her mother.

"Ciddy, calm down. I swear you have your father's flair for the dramatic."

Ciddy jumped down from the sofa and skipped across the room. Constance looked out the window at the empty street.

Moments later, C.B. DeMille, entered the apartment with one hand behind his back. He allowed a little wooden doll to peek her head from behind his back and Ciddy shrieked with joy.

"She's beautiful," Ciddy said as she brought the doll to her face and looked up at DeMille lovingly.

DeMille, Constance, and Ciddy sat at the dinner table. DeMille stuffed his napkin into his shirt collar so it hung down his shirt like a bib. Constance did a double take and gave DeMille a disapproving look as she placed her own napkin on her lap. DeMille got the hint and moved his napkin to the proper position.

"Alright. Let's bow our heads," he said.

Constance and Ciddy bowed their heads and clasped their hands in prayer.

DeMille began, "Dear Lord in heaven. I thank you for all your gifts. Bless this wonderful meal and the lovely hands that prepared it."

Later that evening, DeMille poked his head into Ciddy's bedroom. Ciddy slept with her arm around the wooden doll. DeMille entered quietly and kissed her on the forehead.

Constance stood in the living room as DeMille approached her. "How can we afford toys when we barely have food in the house?" she asked.

"Have faith, my love. Sit, and let me rub your feet."

Constance sat down on the sofa, kicked off her shoes and presented her feet to DeMille.

"Imagine if suddenly you could have anything your heart desires," DeMille said.

"There you go with your stories again. Now stop. You know how easily entranced I can get when you start letting your imagination run wild," said Constance. She melted to the gentle touch of his hands as he caressed her feet.

CHAPTER 3

RITZ-CARLTON, 1913

DeMille entered the elegant Ritz Carlton Hotel, looking out of place in his cheap suit. A 32-piece orchestra played in the background. The banner behind the band read THE RITZ-CARLTON ORCHESTRA - PAUL BERLINER, DIRECTOR. Paul Berliner, handsome, slicked back hair, directed a stirring ragtime piece. Ferns in huge brass pots surrounded the large dining room.

DeMille joined Jesse L. Lasky and Sam Goldfish at their table. Jesse was short. Sam was tall, heavy-set and round faced. Lasky saw DeMille arrive and smiled. "C.B., my good man. This is my brother-in-law, Sam Goldfish. He sells gloves."

DeMille reached over to shake hands with Goldfish.

Goldfish stood and gave DeMille a hearty double grip handshake. He spoke with a heavy

Yiddish accent. "Jesse here tells me you're a wonderfully talented man."

The men took their seats and DeMille replied, "For a short guy, Jesse knows how to tell tall tales."

Goldfish laughed and nodded. "Once you can fake sincerity, you've got it made."

The orchestra music reached a crescendo as well dressed men and women dined and danced in the background.

DeMille turned to Goldfish, "Glove salesman, eh?"

Goldfish slapped Jesse on the back. "Make fewer better! That's my motto and I stand by it."

DeMille curiously looked at them both. "Well, I know nothing about gloves."

Lasky and Goldfish snickered.

Lasky said, "We're here to talk pictures -- moving pictures." He paused a moment. "We're gonna make 'em in out west - in California."

DeMille chuckled. "Will never happen. Who ever heard of making moving pictures in California?"

Lasky smiled. A waiter brought the men their extravagant dinner. As the waiter turned, he bumped into Julia Faye, smart, young, and beautiful, with long, wavy brown hair, brown eyes. Water from the waiter's pitcher splashed against her red silk dress.

Julia spoke with a sultry Southern drawl. "For heaven's sakes," she said, wiping her dress with her hands.

All three men instantly darted up and offered their napkins. Julia snatched the napkin from DeMille's hand and patted the wet spot on her dress, next to her breast. Then she pulled out a cigarette from a fancy silver case.

"Pardon me, gentlemen. But can one of you boys light a lady's fire?"

DeMille, Lasky, and Goldfish simultaneously struck matches. Julia leaned in to DeMille. "Thank you, sugar."

Orchestra music drowned the din of the dining crowd.

Later, the men finished their dinner and lit up big Cuban cigars.

"So, what do you think of Sam's idea?" Lasky asked DeMille.

Goldfish grabbed two of the menus and handed them to DeMille and Lasky. He turned the first menu upside down and took out a pen. Goldfish said, "A verbal agreement isn't worth the paper it's written on."

Goldfish handed the menu and the pen to Lasky. Lasky scribbled something on the back of the menu and looked up. Lasky said, "The Jesse

Lasky Feature Play Company. Good name since I'm the only one here with name recognition. And Sam, with his sales background will be in charge of distribution. That leaves you, C.B., as Director General, with total creative control."

Lasky handed the menu back to Goldfish, who read it to himself slowly and nodded approvingly. Goldfish handed it to DeMille.

DeMille read Lasky's scribbling and shook his head. "Total creative control. Sounds wonderful, except for one thing." He paused. "I know nothing about making pictures."

Goldfish slapped Lasky on the shoulder and the two men busted out laughing. Goldfish said, "Everything you need to know about making pictures you can learn in one day."

The men exited the hotel, laughing. Goldfish stopped to light a cigar. He offered cigars to DeMille and Lasky, who also lit up. The smoke rose and shimmered against the moonlit night. They looked up to see the downtown sky alighted with a spectacular fire. Sirens wailed in the distance.

DeMille, Goldfish, and Lasky made their way down the street, where the blaze leapt and danced from a nearly destroyed office building.

Fire trucks and firefighters surrounded the building, dowsing the flames with hoses and buckets of water.

DeMille watched a small man, with his hands in the pockets of his mink overcoat, standing absolutely still in the excited, milling crowd.

DeMille nudged Lasky and pointed toward the man in mink. "Look at that man. He hasn't moved a muscle since we have been here. He has something to do with this fire. I don't know what, but I am sure of it."

Lasky looked at the man and nodded his head. "You're right," he said. "That's Adolph Zukor, head of Famous Players. That was his studio building."

DeMille approached the small, thin Zukor, extending his hand. "Mr. Zukor. I'm sorry about your studio."

Zukor continued looking straight ahead. He kept his hands in his pockets. "We'll build a better one," he said.

CHAPTER 4

DEMILLE APARTMENT

Ciddy played with her wooden doll. Constance sat on the sofa beside her. "Look, mother. Dolly is a picture star." Ciddy manipulated the doll's hands and bounced the doll up and down on her knee. She pretended the doll was talking. "I am Cleopatra. Queen of the Nile."

Constance said, "That's very nice, dear. But you know that in pictures, the actors don't really speak out loud. They act."

Ciddy bounced the doll up and down on her knee and silently mouthed the words, "I am Cleopatra. Queen of the Nile."

DeMille entered the apartment and Ciddy tossed the doll down on the sofa. She jumped up and gave him a big hug. "Father! I'm teaching Dolly to be the star of a picture show."

Ciddy grabbed the doll and bounced her up and down in the air, pretending to make her talk. "I am Cleopatra. Queen of the Nile."

DeMille chuckled and clapped his hands in applause. "Oh, that's very good. Dolly is a very fine actress, my dear. In fact, I may just put her in one of my own pictures."

Ciddy clapped her hands. "Your own pictures?"

"Oh, Cecil," Constance interrupted. "Don't tease the girl like that."

"Who's teasing? That's what I've been waiting to tell you, my love. Something wonderful is happening," DeMille said.

Ciddy jumped up and down on the couch. "What is it, father?"

DeMille sat on the couch and motioned for Ciddy to come to him. Ciddy stopped jumping and climbed up on DeMille's lap.

"I'm going into the picture business," he said. "Everything is all worked out and I've been offered a job as Director General." He looked to Constance for her reaction.

Constance crossed her arms in front of her and looked away.

"I believe that this is going to be grand," DeMille said. DeMille slid Ciddy off his lap and stood to his feet. He paced the room as he spoke. "Imagine. What if you had this deep yearning to do something so profound and so far reaching that you could barely utter such a vision?"

"You're talking in riddles, Cecil," Constance replied. "Come on. Tell me what's going on?"

"I'm going into partnership with Jesse and his brother-in-law, a Mr. Goldman, or Goldblatt, or something like that." DeMille took a seat on the sofa. Constance and Ciddy joined him.

"So Mr. Lasky and this other man you barely met are going to put up all the money?" Constance wasn't convinced.

"Yes, more or less. Well, something like that. They've agreed to cover my share of the initial investment until we make a profit. Naturally, I'll need to pay my way to California. That's where we're going to set up shop."

"California? Who ever heard of making pictures in California? From what I hear there's nothing in California but desert and a few scattered orange groves."

"I know it all sounds crazy, but I have a vision. I need you to have faith in me. I promise not to let you down."

Constance grabbed DeMille and put her arms around him. She held him tightly, resting her head on his shoulder.

"I do have faith in you darling," she said.

Ciddy reached over and put her arms around both of them.

"So when should we pack our things?" Constance asked.

"But, I thought you understood," said DeMille.

Constance backed away from DeMille and stood to her feet. She put her hands on her hips. "Understood? Understood what? Cecil?"

DeMille rose and placed his hand on her shoulder. "Constance, my darling. You know that there's nothing that I care more about than you and Ciddy, and if I could take you both with me I would."

"What? You think you're going to go gallivanting across the continent and leave us here to fend for ourselves? I won't stand for it. No Cecil, please don't do this." Constance pounded DeMille's chest with her fists.

Ciddy began to cry. She jumped up and tugged on Constance's dress. "Stop it!" she cried.

Constance pushed Ciddy's hand away. "Ciddy, go to your room!"

DeMille tried to reassure Ciddy. "It's okay honey. Your mother and I are just talking about my trip."

Ciddy looked up at Constance. "I don't understand. Is father going away?"

"No, baby. Your father isn't going

anywhere." Constance turned and walked away. Ciddy grabbed DeMille's leg.

Constance brushed her hair as she prepares for bed. DeMille stood behind her with his hands in his pockets. "I was thinking that as soon as we turn our first profit, I would buy us a big house with a yard in the front and back. With trees.

"What do we need with a big house?" Constance asked. "You know what the doctor said."

"What do doctors know? Anyway, we could adopt."

Constance threw her brush at the mirror, breaking it. "Cecil. Will you stop? Please stop! Stop!"

Constance broke down crying. DeMille reached out and put his hand on her shoulder. "Darling, I'm sorry. You're right. It was a silly idea. I don't know anything about the picture business. I'll tell Jesse the deal is off. I'm sure we'll be fine right where we are."

Thunder echoed in the distance and hard rain crashed against the window. Water dripped from the ceiling onto the bed. DeMille grabbed a pan to catch the dripping rain.

The next day Constance gathered the family silver into a wooden case and handed it to DeMille. She said, "Do what you think is right and I will be with you."

DeMille held Constance in his arms. "Just don't forget about me while I'm gone," DeMille whispered in her ear.

Constance shook her head. "Don't be silly, darling," she said. How could I ever forget the one and only true love in my life?"

DeMille kissed Constance gently on the lips.

Ciddy entered the room rubbing her eyes. She looked up at her father with tears in her eyes. "You won't leave us will you?"

DeMille bent down and picked her up. She wrapped her little arms around his neck and kissed him on the cheek.

DeMille took a deep breath and let it out in a slow sigh. "I know that this is hard for you to understand right now, but please just trust me for now. I'll send for you and mother as soon as I can."

DeMille entered the pawnshop and placed a silver set on the counter. Simpson, the middle-aged owner, counted out a stack of cash.

DeMille stepped onto the train and waved goodbye to Constance and Ciddy. Constance wiped a tear from her eye and waved goodbye. The train whistle blew and the train chug, chug, chugged away from the station.

Ciddy ran after the train with her arms outstretched. "Don't leave us, Daddy!"

Constance ran out and grabbed Ciddy, picking her up in her arms. "Your father isn't leaving us, baby. He's just going to prepare a place for us. We'll be with him soon."

Ciddy turned toward the moving train and gave another little wave toward her father. "I love you!"

DeMille blew a soft kiss from the open door as the train headed down the track, leaving behind a wake of smoke, and then disappearing into the horizon.

CHAPTER 5

TRAIN

DeMille, Lasky, Goldfish, and actor Dusty Farnum took their seats on the train. Lasky leaned over to DeMille. "Once we get you set up in California, Sam and I will head back to New York to run the finance and distribution. You'll have total creative control of the direction of the film."

"This is the first time I've been west of the Mississippi," said DeMille. "I hear California's rugged territory. There's nothing but desert and a few orange groves."

Goldfish laughed. "What do you know from rugged? California's a sunny paradise," he said. "Like heaven on earth. You'll love it. Guaranteed."

DeMille, Lasky, Goldfish and Dusty stepped off the train in rainy, muddy Los Angeles.

Goldfish slipped in the mud, landing on his face. DeMille and Lasky busted out laughing as Goldfish wiped the mud from his eyes.

"Well, what are you waiting for?" Goldfish yelled. "A little help would be nice. Am I asking too much here? Oy!"

CHAPTER 6

HOLLYWOOD, 1913

Miles of orange groves and rolling hills surrounded scattered farmhouses along dirt roads.

DeMille, Lasky and Goldfish stood in front of an old barn. The owner, Jacob Stern, chewed on a piece of straw.

"I'll let you fellers rent the barn for two hundred and fifty dollars a month, and that's a good price, but only on one condition," Stern said.

"And what would that be Mr. Stern?" DeMille asked.

Stern led the men inside the barn and pointed to a carriage and several horses in stables along the side. "After all," he said, "they were here first." The horses whinnied and looked DeMille up and down with mild curiosity.

DeMille watched as Lasky nailed up a sign that read: LASKY FEATURE PLAY COMPANY.

DeMille entered the barn, wearing a pair of Bermuda shorts and low cut shoes. A huge rattlesnake met him inside the doorway as he nearly stepped on the serpent's head. He froze in his tracks as the snake hissed and slithered away. DeMille let out a slow sigh of relief and exclaimed, "A man can't even walk around his own studio without being attacked by vipers."

DeMille looked down at his shoes and shook his head. "These just won't do."

Dressed in high boots, jodhpurs, and carrying a big megaphone, DeMille started shooting The Squaw Man. Lead actor Dusty Farnum, handsome, 20's was dressed in western attire as he stood facing the camera. Henry Wilcoxen, 13, rugged and smart, marked the scene with the clapper. "The Squaw Man. Scene one. Take one," the young Wilcoxen shouted.

DeMille stood to his feet and lifted his megaphone. "Action!"

Later that evening DeMille approached Henry Wilcoxen. "You did good kid. What's your name?"

Wilcoxen replied, "Henry Wilcoxen, sir."

DeMille looked the boy over and said, "Stick with it and never let anybody tell you that you can't do something. Think big and you'll make it big."

DeMille rode his horse home from work when suddenly he heard the sound of gunshots fired in his direction. The horse bucked, knocking DeMille onto the ground. He looked around but didn't see anybody.

Inside the Alexandria Hotel that night DeMille cleaned his big pistol.

Riding back toward the barn, DeMille heard gunshots. Bang! Bang! Bang! More bullets whizzed by his head. DeMille jumped off his horse and chased the shooter through the woods. DeMille fired a shot in the direction of the shooter but found no sign of anyone. Gone without a trace.

DeMille held his pistol at the ready as he looked out the window of his hotel room.

The early sunlight was dim as DeMille entered the Barn. A ruffle beneath his feet - He reached down and discovered...something strewn all over the room. He picked up the unraveled film...Completely ruined. He fell to his knees.

DeMille stormed out of the barn, film in one hand, his gun in the other. "Who did this? Who did this?"

He crumpled the film in his fist. Lasky approached and put his hand on DeMille's shoulder. "It's Zukor's boys from New York. We can't fight them," he said.

"If they want a fight. We'll give it to them," said DeMille. "We'll hit them hard. Right where it hurts."

Goldfish said, "I tell you that Adolph Zukor thinks he owns the picture business. I never liked him and I always will."

DeMille balled his fist. "Our success is the best revenge."

Inside the barn, DeMille huddled around a table with Dusty Farnum, Lasky, Goldfish, and young Henry Wilcoxen. DeMille held up a handful of the ruined film. He looked around the room with curious contempt. "I refuse to be intimidated," he said as he tossed the film down on the table.

"What are we going to do?" Lasky asked.

DeMille looked Lasky in the eye sternly. "As God is my witness, we're going to make this picture. And then we're going to make another and another and another!"

DeMille stood to his feet and headed toward the door. He stopped and turned toward the men. "Now let's get back to work."

DeMille rounded the cast and crew back to their starting placed. "OK, everybody. Places, people!"

Several Native Americans with full headdress pulled up in a pickup truck. They jumped out and took their positions. The lovely Princess Red Wing smiled at DeMille adoringly.

Later, Dusty Farnum picked up a discarded piece of ruined film from the ground and touched it with a lit cigarette. DeMille watched in horror as it went up in flames instantly. Farnum looked up at DeMille. "We need to do something to protect our assets. We lose this film, we lose everything."

DeMille showed what remained of the film to Lasky. "I want an extra negative of every reel for safekeeping."

"You know that's going to double production costs, right?"

"I don't care how much it costs. All I care about is getting this picture made. Make it happen."

DeMille directed the final scene in *The Squaw Man* with a close up of Dusty Farnum and beautiful actress Winnifred Kingston kissing. DeMille lifted his megaphone. "Cut!

The cast and crew members burst into applause as DeMille stood to his feet and spread his arms in appreciation.

CHAPTER 7

NEW YORK CITY

Irving, heavy set, wearing a bow tie and derby, entered the spacious office and stood in front of a large mahogany desk. The Man behind the desk had his back to Irving. The Man looked out the window smoking a cigar. He wore a flashy diamond ring on his little finger. The man turned around revealing himself as Adolph Zukor.

Zukor took a puff on his cigar. "So what's the latest on this DeMille fellow and his band of renegades in Los Angeles?" He pronounced Los Angeles with a hard g as in game and a long e, like please. Los Anguhleeeze.

Irving shuffled his weight from side to side. "I'm afraid it's not good news, Mr. Zukor. They've finished post-production on a four-reeler. The film is just about ready for distribution."

"We'll just see about that," said Zukor as he took another puff on his cigar and turned his chair back around facing the window.

Inside the barn that night, DeMille slept on a cot holding the film can in one hand and his chrome revolver in the other. Rain poured down through the leaky roof.

Inside the screening room the following day, DeMille screened *The Squaw Man* for top cast members and executives, including Dusty Farnum, Lasky, and Goldfish. The picture jumped up and down off the screen. DeMille and Lasky looked at each other in panic. "Heaven help us," he whispered. DeMille stopped the film. DeMille stood before the stunned audience.

"I'll let you boys straighten this out while I head back to New York and try to keep the money boys from shutting us down," said Lasky as he pushed through the murmuring crowd and exited the room.

DeMille and Goldfish entered the cluttered film lab. Hidden behind rows of projectors and stacks of film cans, emerged Pop Lubin, lanky, wild gray hair. Lubin spoke with a thick German accent. "You must be Mr. DeMille and Mr. Goldfish."

DeMille handed Lubin the film can. "I think we've been sabotaged."

Lubin examined the film, nodded, and broke out laughing. DeMille and Goldfish looked at each other with confusion. "I don't find our situation humorous in the least bit, Mr. Lubin," said DeMille.

"Call me Pop," Lubin replied as he continued to unroll the film, examining the sprocket holes under a magnifying glass. Lubin bust out laughing again and set the reel down on his workbench.

DeMille grew impatient. "Please, Mr. Lubin."

Lubin wagged his finger at DeMille. "Pop. Call me Pop, I said. What's wrong with you young people these days? You don't mind your elders?" Lubin paused. "So tell me Mr. DeMille. Where did you purchase your sprocket puncher?"

"Our other partner, Mr. Lasky purchased it in New York as I recall. He got a very good deal on it actually," DeMille answered.

Lubin examined the film again and nodded. "Let me put it to you this way, gentlemen." Lubin chuckled softly. "You got rooked! Hoodwinked! Bamboozled!" he exclaimed as he laughed loudly and slapped his knee.

"I don't understand," said DeMille.

Lubin grabbed another reel of film from his stack. He held up DeMille's film next to the other reel, revealing how the sprocket holes were mismatched. "Here's your problem," Lubin said, pointing to the mismatched holes. "You probably used a British sprocket puncher to make these holes. That's why they're mismatched. What you need is a machine made right here in the good old U.S. of A."

Lubin turned to a bench behind him and blew the dust off an old machine. "As a matter of fact, I just so happen to have a spare one right here. I can let you have it real cheap."

"Can you fix the film, Pop?" asked DeMille.

Lubin chuckled again and shook his head. "Can I fix it? Sure, no problem. Hand me that glue over there."

Inside the theater that night, the audience thundered in applause at the premiere of *The Squaw Man*.

DeMille and Goldfish stood in front of the theater after the premier, shaking hands repeatedly and hugging each other in congratulations for a job well done.

The next morning Zukor looked at the New York Times headline that read: SQUAW MAN BIG HIT! He threw the newspaper on his desk and looked up, shouting. "I thought you told me DeMille was finished? Some finish. Now he thinks he's a big shot out there in Los Angeles. Well he won't get away with it, I say. Now what are you going to do about it?"

Zukor glared as Irving stood on the other side of his desk.

Irving shifted nervously, wringing his hands. "I have another idea, sir."

"You and your big fat ideas. If I had a nickel for every one of your good ideas, I'd be in hock up to my eyeballs."

Irving scratched his head. "I've brought someone I think you might want to meet," he said and motioned toward the door. Jesse Lasky entered the room, hat in hand.

CHAPTER 8

DEMILLE HOME

DeMille gave Constance an elegant silver set, much larger than the one he originally took to the pawnshop. Constance smiled widely and fondly.

DeMille and Goldfish sat and ate at the elegant Brown Derby restaurant. DeMille said, "I'm sorry things didn't work out with you and Blanche. She seemed like such a lovely girl."

Goldfish wiped his mouth with his napkin. "I'm learning to regret it myself. The woman had such lovely hands I was going to have a bust made of them. I tell you a bachelor's life is no life for a single man."

Julia Faye, Norma Desmond and the very young Virginia Rappe sat together at a nearby table, giggling and smoking cigarettes. Julia pointed toward the table where DeMille and Goldfish sat. She whispered something to Norma and they both giggled.

Zukor, wearing his trademark mink coat, entered the restaurant, flanked by Lasky and Irving. Julia and Norma looked away and quieted down. Zukor and Lasky approached DeMille and Goldfish at the table. DeMille and Goldfish begin to rise but Zukor interrupted them. "Don't bother to get up gentlemen. I'll make this short and sweet."

Lasky stood nervously by Zukor's side, averting his eyes away from DeMille and Goldfish.

"What's this all about?" DeMille asked.

Zukor put a cigar in his mouth. Lasky lit it for him. Irving stood silently in the background. Zukor took a puff on his cigar. "I'm here to announce the formation of Famous Players-Lasky Corporation." He paused a moment for affect.

"On second thought, I will take a seat." Zukor took a seat and blew smoke in DeMille's direction.

DeMille stifled a cough. He glared at Lasky. "Jesse. What's the meaning of this?"

Zukor interjected, leaving Lasky with his mouth hanging open. "The meaning is that Mr.

Lasky and I have signed an agreement to merge our companies. Boys, meet your new boss," Zukor said pointing to himself with both thumbs.

Lasky took an audible breath and looked to Zukor for approval before speaking. Zukor gave him a miniscule nod. "I know this is all rather sudden," Lasky began, "but, I assure you that this is the best thing for the company. Mr. Zukor has gained control of nearly 80 percent of all film distribution in the country."

"But, I'm in charge of distribution," Goldfish exclaimed. "We had a deal."

Zukor poked Lasky in the arm with his bony index finger. "I thought you had already taken care of this part. Go ahead and tell him."

Lasky hesitated, looking around nervously.

Goldfish looked at Lasky with bewilderment. "What part is this?"

Zukor stuck the cigar in his mouth. "The part where you're fired," he said. "Kaput. Now get lost. Scram!"

Zukor waved his hand in Goldfish's face dismissively.

Goldfish sat there in stunning silence for a moment. "What's with this crazy talk?" he asked, looking at Zukor in disbelief. "You can't fire me." Goldfish looked to Jessie for a reality check. "Can he Jesse?"

Lasky shrugged his shoulders and nodded his head. "Sorry, Sam," he said. "It's just business, you know?"

Goldfish stood up and slowly, and methodically folded his napkin, setting it neatly on the table. He smiled slyly, turning to DeMille. "Beware of men in mink."

Zukor stroked his mink coat as Goldfish eyed him with contempt. Zukor puffed again on his cigar and blew the smoke in Goldfish's face.

Goldfish pointed his finger in Zukor's face. "I said I never liked you and I always will. Go ahead and include me out. What do I care?" he said as he calmly strolled out of the restaurant.

DeMille, Lasky, and Zukor sat quietly for a moment, DeMille glaring at Zukor. Zukor turned to DeMille. "From now on, you don't write a script, you don't shoot a scene, you don't make a picture without my approval," he said before putting out his cigar in Goldfish's plate.

Zukor put his fists together and made a snapping motion, looking DeMille dead in the eye. "DeMille, I can break you like that," he said. Zukor quietly stood to his feet and walked out, Lasky and Irving obediently following behind him.

A stunned DeMille took a drink. An elegant

and beautiful African American woman took the stage and sang a haunting blues solo.

Julia, Norma, and Virginia watched silently as DeMille gulped down the rest of his drink. He slammed the glass down on the table.

Julia, Norma, and Virgie approach DeMille's table. "We heard you were in the picture business."

DeMille waved them away in disgust. "Not anymore!" he shouted and he hung his head and then banged the glass on the table repeatedly until it shattered in his hand.

CHAPTER 9

THE BARN

Lasky hammered a sign above the barn door that read:

FAMOUS PLAYERS-LASKY CORPORATION

Inside the DeMille home, Constance changed the bandages on DeMille's bleeding hand. "I've had it, Constance. It's no use kidding myself anymore."

"Darling, what are you saying?"

"My father always wanted me to follow in his footsteps. Maybe I should have listened to him."

Constance rubbed DeMille's neck. Your father was a wonderful preacher, dear. And I'm sure he's as proud as he could be looking down at you commanding your own wild pulpit," she said. She stood up and walked to the bookcase where she reached for a well-worn Bible. She handed the Bible to DeMille. "Now enough of this foolish talk and read me a story."

DeMille thumbed through the Bible and smiled. "What'll it be?"

"Exodus."

CHAPTER 10

ROSE OF THE RANCHO SET

The set was an old west background with horses tied in front of a saloon. DeMille sat in front of the Barn in his director's chair, ordering around the cast and crew as they shot a scene from the film *Rose of the Rancho*.

Suddenly a caravan of cars and trucks pulled up in front of the location. Jeanie Macpherson dressed in a long blue dress and fancy hat, barged onto the set with her own small cast and crew, interrupting the shot.

DeMille saw the commotion and jumped up from his director's seat. "Cut! Cut! Cut!"

Jeanie and her crew began setting up their own cameras and equipment. DeMille ran over and pushed her crew members back, knocking over one of their cameras. "What in God's name is going on here? Don't you know I'm in the middle of making a picture?" he yelled. "Now get out of here before I have you all thrown out. Who do you think you are?"

Jeanie looked DeMille in the eye and put her hands on her hips. A cigarette hung from her lips. "The name's Jeanie Macpherson and I'm the set manager for D.W. Griffith's picture. I'm afraid you'll have to move your equipment until we're done."

"OK. Wait here," said DeMille. He turned and marched into the Barn.

Moments later, DeMille came running out of the Barn and chased Jeanie and her crew off the set with a shotgun.

Jeanie and her crewmembers jumped back in their vehicles and hightailed it out of there, leaving clouds of dust in their wake. DeMille fired the shotgun over their heads. BOOM! BOOM! BOOM!

TWO DAYS LATER

BANG! BANG! BANG!

DeMille sat at his desk writing in his red notebook. He ignored the person banging on the door as he continued writing. Jeanie barged in and stood in front of DeMille with her hands on her hips. "Mr. DeMille, I demand an apology."

DeMille sighed and continued writing in his

notebook without acknowledging her.

"And I'll have you know that I'm not only a scenario writer and director, but I'm a great actress as well," she said. Jeanie lit up a cigarette before continuing. "As a matter of fact, I'm one of the greatest actresses you'll ever see. Even better than that over-rated tramp Norma Desmond."

DeMille glanced up at her briefly, and then continued with his work, without saying a word. Jeanie tossed her cigarette on the floor and stomped it out with her foot. DeMille continued to ignore her.

"Well!" Jeanie stormed out in a huff.

Two weeks later, the glamorous Norma Desmond slowly descended a spiral staircase.

Jeanie quietly entered the set and stood in the wings.

"Cut!" DeMille shouted.

Norma walked up to DeMille and smiled.

"Good job, Norma," he said.

Norma exited as Henry Wilcoxen turned off the spotlights. DeMille headed towards his office and Jeanie followed him inside.

"I'm still waiting on that apology Mr. DeMille."

DeMille turns toward Jeanie, startled. Then

he took his seat behind his desk. "I tell you what. I'll pay you twenty-five dollars a week to take dictation."

"Not only are you too stubborn to apologize for nearly killing me and my crew, but now you have the nerve to insult me." Jeanie stomped her foot and slammed her fists into her thighs. She suddenly straightened up and lit a cigarette, trying to regain her composure. "I tell you I won't stand for it. You let me walk out that door one more time and you'll regret it for the rest of your life."

Jeanie took a long drag from her cigarette. She exhaled as a tear slowly traced down her cheek. "I'm a wonderful actress, Mr. DeMille and I can write. I promise you're going to love me. Please, you've got to give me just one chance. Please, I'm begging you. I need this. Please."

Jeanie hung her head, sobbing desperate, pitiful tears.

DeMille sighed and rubbed his chin. "I'll pay you ten dollars for one day's work as an actress. Be here tomorrow morning at 8:00 a.m. And don't be late."

Jeanie looked up and wiped her eyes with her sleeve.

"Ten bucks? You expect me to work a whole

day for ten lousy bucks? What kind of girl do you think I am? Why I'm worth ten times that much!"

"Take it or leave it."

Jeanie took another drag from her cigarette and blew smoke rings. "Well, alright, I guess I'll take it. But consider this a big favor. You're going to realize that Jeanie Macpherson is worth her weight in gold. You'll see. I guarantee it." Then she skipped out of the room humming *Hooray for Hollywood*.

DeMille chuckled and shook his head.

Norma walked up to DeMille with a big smile, making exotic movements with her hands in front of her face. "I'm ready for my close up, Mr. DeMille."

DeMille directed the close up shot on Norma as Jeanie walked through the background, smiling for the camera, trying to steal the scene.

"Cut!"

Jeanie sauntered into DeMille's office. "See? I told you I was good," she said.

DeMille reached into his pocket. "Here you go." DeMille handed Jeanie a check for ten dollars. She stared at the check for a moment and looked up at DeMille in disbelief. "What?

This is only ten dollars!"

"Yes. Well, that was our agreement."

Jeanie stomped her feet, tossing the check back on the desk. "You know that I'm worth ten times that amount. My fee is one hundred dollars a day or nothing." She crossed her arms in front of her and tapped her foot impatiently.

"Very well then, if you insist," said DeMille as he snatched up the check, putting it back in his pocket.

CHAPTER 11

FAMOUS PLAYERS

Zukor and Lasky approached DeMille in front of the barn. "Good news, DeMille. I've just purchased another distribution company and merged it with Famous Players – Lasky. Rolled up everything into one big ball of wax. This is going to be big, I tell you. Big."

Zukor handed Lasky a sign, a hammer and a couple of nails. Lasky pulled down the old Famous Players – Lasky sign and nailed the new sign in its place. The sign above the barn door now read:

PARAMOUNT PICTURES

TWO YEARS LATER

The ornate sign above the gated studio entrance read:

PARAMOUNT PICTURES

Jeanie sat at her desk typing on the Royal typewriter. Her fingers hunted and pecked the words: THE END. She ripped the paper out of the typewriter and placed it at the bottom of a manuscript. The cover page read *THE UNAFRAID*.

She grabbed the script and ran to the adjacent office. The sign on the door read: CECIL B. DEMILLE, DIRECTOR-GENERAL. Jeanie dashed into DeMille's office and handed him the script.

DeMille took the script and sat back in his chair as he read the first few pages. He flipped through the script, skimming through the pages randomly until he came to the end. He picked up a red pencil and went back to the beginning marking up each page. "Come back in an hour," he said.

Jeanie stormed out of the office, slamming the door behind her.

One hour later, Jeanie stood back in front of DeMille's desk, nervously smoking a cigarette. "Well, what did you think?"

DeMille extended the script in Jeanie's direction and flipped through it so she could see the red markings on every page. "What I have crossed out I didn't like. What I haven't crossed out I'm dissatisfied with."

"What?"

"Quite frankly, Miss Macpherson, you write like a plumber. Nobody wants to see page after page of furniture descriptions. It reads more like a Sears Catalog than a motion picture scenario. I want to see a love story. Show me the heart. Show me the love." DeMille tossed the script at Jeanie and it fell apart, pages scattering in all directions. "Now go back and rewrite it with heart. And have it on my desk by noon tomorrow."

Jeanie gathered the scattered pages, crawling on her hands and knees across the floor. DeMille ignored her as he wrote in his notebook.

Inside Jeanie's office that night, Jeanie clickity clacked on the typewriter. The clock on the wall chimed midnight, then 2:00 a.m., then 4:00 a.m. DeMille entered Jeanie's office and saw her sleeping on the floor. He tenderly lifted her to the sofa and her shoe fell off. He laid his coat across Jeanie's shoulders as she slept.

The next day Jeanie sat at the dinner table at the lavish DeMille home. Constance brought out the dessert, a large chocolate mousse. "Ah. This looks wonderful," said DeMille. "Wonderful, I tell you."

Constance served DeMille's plate first. She passed by Jeanie without acknowledging her then proceeded to serve the four children, Ciddy, 10, Katherine, 6, John, 5, and Richard, 4. DeMille and Constance had adopted Katherine, John, and Richard soon after settling in Los Angeles.

Constance served herself then took her seat next to DeMille, leaving Jeanie's dessert plate still empty. DeMille got up and served Jeanie's plate. "Thank you, C.B," said Jeanie. "It looks delicious."

Ciddy made faces and mocked Jeanie behind her back as Katherine, John, and Richard burst into laughter. DeMille saw what's going on and yelled, "Children. Go to your rooms. I've had about enough of your disorderliness for one night. Now off with you."

"We haven't finished our dessert," Ciddy whined.

Constance loyally stood by her husband. "You heard your father. Now off to bed."

Ciddy stuck her tongue out at Jeanie and ran from the dining room, followed by the other children, laughing all the way upstairs.

Constance glared at Jeanie with silent contempt. She yawned and patted her mouth. "My, it is getting late. We should be getting to bed soon ourselves."

Later that evening DeMille followed Constance up the stairs. Constance entered the bedroom and slammed the door in his face.

CHAPTER 12

AMBASSADOR HOTEL

DeMille and Jeanie entered the Ambassador Hotel arm in arm. They bumped into director Desmond Taylor, actress Mabel Normand, actor Roscoe "Fatty" Arbuckle in the hotel lobby.

"Ah, C.B. my good man," said Desmond, greeting him with open arms. "Fancy meeting you here. How goes it?"

DeMille looked around the lobby to see who else might notice him. He scratched his head. "Desmond. I'm here for a meeting. Yes, that's it." He pointed to Jeanie. "This is Miss Jeanie Macpherson here. She's my head scenario writer."

"Sure she is," said Desmond as he gave DeMille a wink.

Desmond reached for Jeanie's hand, kissing her on the wrist. "Desmond Taylor at your service."

Jeanie blushed. "Charmed. I'm sure."

Arbuckle, stumbling drunk, insinuated himself into the mix as the sixteen-year-old starlet, Virginia Rappe stepped up from behind grabbing him by the arm. "We're headed up to San Francisco tonight for a big bash," he slurred. "You should come with us, C.B. It's gonna be lots of fun. Plenty of dames, cards, booze. You name it. Anything goes."

"Afraid we can't join you tonight Roscoe. We're here on business," DeMille said.

Arbuckle laughed and did a little jig. "Oh, yeah. Monkey business. I get it." Arbuckle winked at DeMille and gave DeMille a nudge with his elbow.

"Now, if you'll excuse us. We really do have a meeting to attend to," DeMille replied.

Arbuckle grabbed DeMille by the arm. "Oh, where oh where are my manners?" he asked. "Let me introduce you to my new girlfriend, Miss Virgie Rappe. I'm going to make her famous." He gazed at Virgie adoringly. "Aren't I baby?

"Anything you say, Daddy," she said as she ran her fingers through his hair. "I'm all yours."

Arbuckle reached over and gave Virgie a sloppy wet kiss on the mouth.

Later that night, police led Fatty Arbuckle out of the St. Francis Hotel in handcuffs. Ambulance workers carried Virgie's body out on a stretcher. Reporters and photographers crowded in. Cameras flashed.

DeMille stood in front of the Barn reading the Los Angeles Herald. The headlines read: **ARBUCKLE ARRESTED IN ORGY DEATH.**

The voice of a radio announcer droned in the background. "Comedic actor, Roscoe "Fatty" Arbuckle was arrested tonight at the St. Francis Hotel in San Francisco for the alleged rape and murder of underage starlet, Miss Virginia Rappe."

DeMille looked up toward the sky.

CHAPTER 13

AEROPLANE

The sun shined brightly over the horizon as DeMille took Jeanie for a cruise in his private plane. The side of the plane read: MERCURY AVIATION.

"You know I own an entire fleet of aeroplanes. One of these days people will fly back and forth the country like it was nothing."

"Oh, C.B. don't be silly. Aeroplanes are just for fun. Nobody could really take flying seriously."

The plane flew into a thick fog, heading straight toward a mountainside. DeMille barely saw the mountain and pulled up just in time.

Jeanie clapped her hands as she enjoyed the ride. "You see? Now wasn't that fun? Let's do it again, C.B." She reached over and gave DeMille a big kiss, covering his face as the plane spiraled downward.

Zukor stood next to a sign that read: MERCURY AIRFIELD. He watched from the ground with his hands on his hips as DeMille made a precarious landing.

DeMille and Jeanie exited the plane and Zukor approached.

"You're killing me, DeMille. I've got a business to run and you're out risking your neck in some aeroplane. I'm paying you to make pictures, not to run an airline." Dozens of planes marked MERCURY AVIATION lined the field.

CHAPTER 14

PARAMOUNT STUDIOS

The next morning, DeMille and Jeanie entered the studio gates of the elaborate, new Paramount Studios. DeMille and Jeanie walked through the studio hallway toward their conjoined offices. A pair of secretaries whispered and giggled as the couple passed.

That evening, Constance set the dinner table. "Children! Come to supper. Ciddy! Bring your brothers and sister down here at once."

Constance, Ciddy, Katherine, John and Richard sat around the table together for dinner. An empty place was set at the head of the table. Ciddy looked up at her mother. "Where's father? Isn't he coming home for supper tonight?"

"Your father is at another one of his meetings, dear. We shall eat supper without him. Now let's say grace." Everyone bowed their heads and closed their eyes. Constance began,

"Dear Lord. Bless this meal and our family."

Ciddy interrupted, "And bless father too."

Constance looked at Ciddy disapprovingly. "Amen."

The children replied in unison. "Amen."

DeMille arrived home late that night when everyone was asleep, except for Constance, who sat waiting in the living room. "Sorry darling. Another meeting with the studio boss," he said.

"Do you think I'm stupid? I can smell her." Constance marched upstairs and DeMille chased after her. She stormed into the bedroom, slamming the door in his face.

DeMille leaned his forehead on the bedroom door and whispered, "God, forgive me."

He tiptoed into the children's bedrooms and kissed them all good night as they slept and he went to his separate room at the other end of the hall where he wept.

CHAPTER 15

HOLLYWOOD PARTY

DeMille and Constance wove their way through a fancy Hollywood party. Constance left DeMille's side to speak with a group of Hollywood wives.

Handsome actor Wallace Reid approached DeMille with the beautiful, young Julia Faye, now in her mid 20's.

DeMille greeted his old friend. "Wallace, my good man, who is this charming young lady?"

"Allow me to introduce you to the young actress I've been telling you about," said Reid. "Meet Miss Julia Faye."

DeMille took Julia's hand and kissed it. "Pleased to make your acquaintance, Miss Faye."

"The pleasure is all mine, sugar," she replied with her sultry Southern drawl. "Haven't we met somewhere before?" She remembered

DeMille lighting her fire at the Ritz-Carlton.

"Ah, yes," he replied. "You do look familiar. In fact, I read an article that stated you have the prettiest feet in America."

Julia blushed, and then gently lifted her foot from her shoe. "Well aren't you just as sweet as a mint julep in July?"

DeMille looked down as Julia wiggled her toes. "I'll let you be the judge."

Reid nodded his head and turned to leave. "Well, looks like my queue to exit stage right."

DeMille and Julia gazed into each other's eyes with longing and remembering as the rest of the room faded into a blur.

Jeanie emerged from the crowd and eyed the pair with disdain. She lit a cigarette and stormed out of the room. DeMille never noticed that she was there.

On board DeMille's private yacht, *The Seaward*, Jeanie and Julia worked with DeMille on a script. Julia looked at the script page and then looked over at Jeanie. "Well, I think you're wrong," she said. "Dead wrong. I think it stinks."

"Who really cares what you think, because you're not writing are you?"

DeMille interrupted. "Girls! Enough with the

bickering already. I don't have time for any more of this foolishness. We've got a scenario to write."

Jeanie wasn't through yet. "I don't even see why she's here," she said. "What does she know about writing? She can barely act."

Julia stood to her feet. "Well, Jezebel, how about I just write you out of this story altogether?"

Jeanie stood up and moved up face to face with Julia. "You and what army?"

Suddenly, a gust of wind blew pages of notes into the ocean. DeMille jumped to his feet. "My notes!" he shouted and he dove overboard and treaded water as he retrieved the floating sheets of paper.

Julia and Jeanie looked over the bow in astonishment.

Later that night, Jeanie paced back and forth on deck smoking a cigarette, alone. She could hear DeMille and Julia laughing from the Captain's quarters below.

DeMille entertained Julia below deck, rubbing her feet. "You say you love me," said Julia. "Then why do you refuse to divorce Constance and marry me?"

DeMille sat back and took a deep sigh. "Because it would be wrong to divorce

Constance. I couldn't hurt her like that." An awkward silence hung in the air for a moment. "Besides you are, in fact, my true spiritual as well as physical wife. That's all that matters." DeMille took Julia in his arms and pulled her into a passionate kiss.

CHAPTER 16

GRIFFITH PARK

DeMille sat alone on a bench in Griffith Park as Julia approached. Julia lit a cigarette and offered one to DeMille. DeMille gestured "no" with his hand and shook his head. Julia sat down next to him. "C.B. I know this isn't a good time to tell you this. But Momma told me that sometimes a girl just has to say what she's got to say."

"What is it Julia?" he asked.

"I guess there's no easy way to say this, but, I'm in a family way."

"You're what?"

"Sugar, I'm four weeks late and I think we might be pregnant." She rubbed her hand across her belly.

The next morning Constance packed up Ciddy and the other children and exited the DeMille home to a waiting car. DeMille chased her outside. "Constance," he pleaded. "Please don't do this. Don't take the children! Ciddy!"

Ciddy looked back at DeMille. "I don't want to go!"

Constance grabbed Ciddy by the arm and dragged her to the car. "Get in." They drove away.

DeMille stood alone in the driveway and looked up toward heaven as drops of rain began to fall, hiding his tears.

Jeanie and Julia stood at opposite ends of DeMille's office facing each other. "You just stay out of it. It's got nothing to do with you," said Julia.

"Home wrecker!" Jeanie shot back. She picked up an inkwell and threw it at Julia and it shattered into pieces on the wall just as DeMille entered the room.

A few months later DeMille screened the film, *Why Change Your Wife?* Jeanie and Julia watched and fumed as they watched the inkwell scene reenacted.

Later that evening DeMille sat alone at his desk, writing in his notebook. The voice of the announcer filtered through the radio.

"Hollywood film star Desmond Taylor was found dead in his Avalon Courts Apartment this morning. Actress Mabel Normand was arrested on suspicion of murder."

Police led Mabel Normand away in handcuffs. Ambulance workers carried Desmond Taylor's body out on a stretcher.

CHAPTER 17

SEAWARD

DeMille sat on the deck of the Seaward with Julia. "This town has devolved into a cesspool of degeneracy. I've got to do something to raise the standard."

Julia kicked off her shoes.

The following night DeMille entered his home and looked around at the emptiness. He sat at the large dining room table alone with a sandwich on a plate in front of him. He bowed his head in prayer. "Dear Lord. Please bring my family back. I know I've failed you. But please give me a chance to make it up. Lord, have mercy on me, the sinner."

He stood and walked to the window. He looked up toward the night sky, shining with stars. "Tell me what I should do. I don't know what to do."

CHAPTER 18

BEVERLY HILLS HOTEL

DeMille carried a large flower bouquet as he approached the front desk clerk. "Could you please ring Mrs. DeMille's room for me?"

"I'm sorry sir," the clerk replied, "but she left strict instructions not to disturb her with any calls or visitors right now."

DeMille pulled a twenty-dollar bill out of his pocket and handed it to the clerk. "Please do me this one little favor. Tell her it's her husband."

The clerk picked up the phone and dialed. "Good afternoon, Mrs. DeMille. This is Arthur at the front desk. So sorry to bother you, but your husband is here and..." The clerk pulled the phone back from his ear with a pained look on his face and hung up the receiver. He looked at DeMille and shook his head. "I apologize sir, but she doesn't wish to speak with you at this time."

CHAPTER 19

DEMILLE OFFICE

C.B. DeMille sat at his desk reading his Bible. He looked up to see Julia standing at the door. "May I come in?"

DeMille looked up at her. "Julia, where have you been? I've been trying to reach you for the last two weeks."

Julia slowly entered and took a seat. She looked at DeMille for a moment and then hung her head. "You don't have to worry anymore," she said.

DeMille looked at her perplexed. "What do you mean, Julia? What did you do? Please tell me you didn't…"

Julia interrupted. "It was my decision."

DeMille stood to his feet. "What? My God. What do you mean your decision? Julia, what have you done? What about me?"

"It wasn't about you," she said as she broke

down sobbing. "I'm so sorry, C.B. Please forgive me. Please."

DeMille glared at her and shook his head. He folded his arms across his chest and sighed heavily.

Julia jumped up and stormed out of the office.

CHAPTER 20

GRIFFITH PARK

C.B. DeMille sat on a bench in Griffith Park reading his Bible. He looked up to see a red butterfly flutter in front of him and land on the grass for a moment before flying off into the distance.

Inside Paramount Studios later that day, DeMille sat at a conference table with Jeanie. He stood up and began pacing, hands clasped behind his back. "We've got to start looking at everything differently. We've got to think big. Biblical."

"What do you mean, C.B.?"

DeMille stopped pacing. "I'm looking for the next big thing. I have a feeling that we are on the brink of a totally new kind of picture. I need to get a feel for what the public wants."

Jeanie laughed. "The public? What does the

public know about making pictures?"

A newsboy hawked the morning headlines. "Extra! Extra! Read all about it. DeMille offers thousand dollar reward for movie idea." Dozens of people reached out to grab newspapers.

Two mailmen pulled bags of mail from the back of a mail truck behind Paramount Studios.

The mailmen poured out thousands of letters on DeMille's desk.

Later, DeMille and Jeanie sorted through the letters. DeMille opened a letter and read the contents aloud. "A man eating Boy Scout, a cowboy, and an aging Irishman team up to form a jazz trio in Cuba."

They both laughed. Jeanie opened another letter. "A bounty hunter goes on a fishing trip with a homicidal picture director."

DeMille rubbed his chin in thought. "Promising. But, no. What else we got?"

Later that evening, a haggard looking DeMille and Jeanie sat in front a much smaller stack of letters. The trashcan overflowed with crumpled pieces of paper. DeMille made a paper airplane with a discarded letter and tossed it across the room.

Jeanie picked up another envelope and

opened it. As she read the letter, a big smile broke across her face. She stood up. "How about this one C.B.?" Jeanie held up the letter and read it aloud. "You cannot break the Ten Commandments – they will break you."

DeMille liked the idea. "The Ten Commandments?" he asked.

"The Ten Commandments!" Jeanie repeated.

"The Ten Commandments! Why of course. That's a wonderful idea."

DeMille stood in front of Zukor's desk with the letter in hand. "That's a horrible idea," said Zukor.

"How can you say that? We're talking about one of the greatest stories ever told."

Zukor got up from his seat, turned to the window behind him, and looked out toward the bustling city. He turned his back toward DeMille as he continued. "Old men wearing tablecloths and beards?" Zukor turned and walked around the desk toward DeMille. He placed his arm on DeMille's shoulder. "Cecil, a picture like that would ruin us."

DeMille wasn't giving up without a fight. "Just think of it," he said. "We'll be the first studio to open and close the Red Sea."

"Maybe," said Zukor. "Or you'll be the first director to open and close Paramount." Zukor lit a cigar and paced around the room finally returning to his seat behind his desk. He took a puff of the cigar and blew smoke rings, imagining them as dollar signs. "So tell me," he began. How much is this baby going to cost me?"

DeMille smiled. "About a million dollars."

Zukor began choking on his own cigar and fell out of his chair. He stumbled to his feet. "What? A million dollars to make a lousy picture? You're crazy. Get out of my office! Now!"

DeMille broke out laughing.

Zukor wasn't laughing as he sat back down. "You think I'm kidding here?" he asked. "I mean it. Get out of here. And stay out until you come to your senses." Zukor paused for a moment, shaking his head in bewilderment. "You're killing me, Cecil. You're killing me!" Zukor threw his cigar at DeMille, barely missing him. The cigar hit the wall and bounced into the wastepaper basket.

DeMille hustled out of Zukor's office as the wastepaper basket burst into flames.

CHAPTER 21

PARAMOUNT STUDIOS

Inside Paramount Studios the next day, DeMille stood in front of his desk, upon which were stacked about a hundred Bibles. Jeanie walked in and did a double take. DeMille looked up and smiled. "Ah. Just who I was looking for," he said. "Jeanie, make sure we get one of these to everyone on the payroll. And make it snappy. We've got a picture to make." DeMille handed Jeanie a stack of Bibles and gestured for her to get hopping.

Jeanie ambled down the hallway with her stack of Bibles and passed them out to everyone she saw.

Lasky entered DeMille's office. "So you're really going through with this Ten Commandments project?" he asked.

"Give me two pages of the Bible and I'll give you a picture," DeMille said, as he handed Lasky a Bible. "Take it wherever you go and read it every day."

Lasky took the Bible and looked at it, curiously. "Maybe I'll get around to it someday."

DeMille rose to his feet and lifted a Bible above his head dramatically. "The Ten Commandments are the foundations of moral decency and virtue. None who defies them shall survive." He slammed the Bible down on his desk.

Zukor slammed *The Ten Commandments* screenplay on his desk. He picked up the phone. "Get me DeMille!" He looked up and saw DeMille peeking into his office.

"Did I hear my name?" DeMille asked.

"Get in here!" said Zukor.

DeMille entered Zukor's office. Zukor flipped through the script. "You bring me a script like this and want money for it? You may as well put your hand in my pocket and steal it. You've got to cut out half of this."

"What do you expect me to make, *The Five Commandments*?"

"How about I just cancel the picture altogether?" Zukor threatened. Zukor took the script in both hands and tried to rip it in half, but it was too thick. Zukor slammed the script back down on his desk.

"I've already got several investors lined up just chomping at the bit," said DeMille. "I'll buy it back and make it myself. Then you can wash your hands of the whole thing, including me." DeMille turned and headed toward the door.

Zukor blinked. "Wait," he said.

DeMille stopped for a moment.

Zukor rose to his feet. "How do you feel about the Red Sea being parted in Los Angeles?"

CHAPTER 22

DEMILLE HOME

DeMille sat alone at the dining room table in his bathrobe eating a sandwich.

Suddenly he heard the sound of a motor running and familiar voices. He looked up as Constance entered home with the children. DeMille stood to his feet. He ran to her. "Darling!"

Ciddy ran to DeMille and jumped into his arms. "Father, I missed you so much."

"I missed you too, precious. You don't know how much I've missed all of you."

"Children," said Constance. "I know that you've all missed your father. But it's getting late and I want you get ready for bed. We'll have plenty of time for talk tomorrow."

DeMille set Ciddy back down.

"But, mother," Ciddy cried. "We just got here."

"Now mind your mother and run along. That goes for all of you." Constance clapped her hands and pointed to the stairway. The children all hugged DeMille and slowly headed upstairs.

Constance turned to DeMille. "A family should stay together," she said. "And now, if you don't mind. I'm rather weary myself." She turned away sharply and headed up the stairs.

DeMille stood at the bottom of the stairs for a moment, and then followed Constance to the bedroom like an eager puppy. Constance slammed the bedroom door in DeMille's face.

CHAPTER 23

HIGHWAY 101

DeMille and his caravan of dozens of cars and trucks headed north on Highway 101. A truck carrying a full size replica of the sphinx stopped on the highway in front of a bridge. The bridge was too low for the sphinx to pass. DeMille stood next to the truck with his hands on his hips talking to the truck driver. The rest of the caravan sat motionless on the highway blocking traffic behind them for miles. Cars honking. People shouting.

Always the director, DeMille ordered everyone to remain calm. "OK," he said. "Let's not lose our heads. There has to be a way to work around this." DeMille looked at the bridge and back at the Sphinx then nodded his head.

Moments later, the now headless Sphinx passed under the bridge, the "head" strapped onto a separate truck following from behind.

DeMille checked Constance and Ciddy into the luxurious Santa Maria Inn.

Heading up Highway 1, the caravan passed a sign that read: WELCOME TO GUADALUPE. Dozens of local Mexican farm workers and their children lined the road, waving and running along side of the trucks.

DeMille and his caravan arrived at the Guadalupe sand dunes. DeMille stood on top of a car in front of his assembled cast and crew and lifted up his megaphone. "Welcome to Camp DeMille. We're here on a divine mission – to make the greatest picture the world has ever seen – The Ten Commandments." The cast and crew broke into roaring applause. "Now let's get to work."

CHAPTER 24

TRAIN STATION

Twenty five hundred extras and forty five hundred animals arrive by train.

Separate mess tents were set up for men and women, seating fifteen hundred people each. A separate tent with a sign that read: KOSHER in English and Hebrew catered to the two hundred orthodox Jews working on the production. Several men sang and performed a traditional Jewish dance in the background.

Uniformed police and police matron corps patrolled the separate camps, chasing men from the female section and vice versa. DeMille's special police drove bootleggers and professional gamblers out of the camp.

DeMille and set designer Paul Iribe, supervised construction of great walls, towering gates, and a row of sphinxes between the dunes. Paul Iribe unveiled his stunning set of the throne room for Rameses II. "Rameses?" DeMille asked. "I thought we were going with Tutankhamen."

"McGaffey's research shows that Tutankhamen had nothing to do with banishing the Israelites," Iribe replied.

"I know that, but I'm talking about name recognition," said DeMille.

DeMille approached cinematographer, Alvin Wykoff who was setting up lighting in the Ramses throne room. Wykoff's young assistant, Pev Marley, early 20's, carried equipment.

"Alvin we need more light on the set," said DeMille. "You're obscuring Paul's background designs."

Wykoff responded with indignation. "This is my vision and I insist on creative control. The lighting must remain low to set the mood."

"You are here to please me. Nothing else on earth matters," said DeMille.

Wykoff folded his arms across his chest defiantly. "I am an artist and I must be free."

Wykoff stood alone on the station platform holding his suitcases as the train whistle signaled its approach and came to a stop in front of him.

CHAPTER 25

TEN COMMANDMENTS SET

DeMille commanded Marley to set up the lighting. "I'm putting you in charge of cinematography. Can you handle it?"

"Yes, Chief. Thanks for putting your trust in me."

"Just do what I say to the letter and we'll get along fine."

Marley nodded and gave DeMille a friendly salute.

DeMille climbed to the top of one of the hundred foot gates with Iribe and looked out over the great expanse of Egyptian architecture spread out over the shimmering sands.

DeMille brought in the familiar Ritz-Carlton Orchestra, with Paul Berliner to play mood music throughout the shooting. The orchestra set up in a special enclosure off camera.

When the Exodus scene started, the extras barely took a few steps when DeMille signaled for everyone to stop by a special fanfare on the trumpets. "Cut!" yelled DeMille. DeMille walked up to a young extra who was chewing gum. "If you want to be a part of this production, you'll spit that gum out right now. The Israelites did not chew gum during the Exodus!"

The extra spit out the gum. "I'm so sorry, Mr. DeMille. It won't happen again."

Another extra giggled. DeMille turned toward her sharply. "And no giggling!"

DeMille returned to his director's chair. Eleven-year-old Ciddy approached DeMille, holding her doll in front of her. She whispered into DeMille's ear and pointed toward the crowd of extras. DeMille saw through his field glasses one little girl with red hair. Ciddy handed DeMille the doll. "Are you sure?" he asked.

Ciddy nodded.

DeMille descended into the crowd of Israelites and spoke to the Little Girl with Red Hair. He returned and approached cinematographer Pev Marley. "Get me a close-up." DeMille watched the little Girl with red hair, smiling and holding Ciddy's doll.

CHAPTER 26

GUADALUPE DUNES

Henry Wilcoxen, now in his early 20's marked the next scene. "Scene 70. Take one." Wilcoxen clapped the slate.

The scene continued with hundreds of chariots heading toward the edge of the sand cliffs. The drivers came to a sudden halt, afraid to proceed. One of the stuntman, a well-built archer with a quiver of arrows on his back, approached DeMille. "The men are saying this scene is too dangerous," the Archer told DeMille. "We can't do it."

DeMille looked at him with disgust then turned to Ciddy. "You want to show them how it's done, Ciddy?"

Moments later, Ciddy rode her pony up to the cliff and made the descent at breakneck speed and without injury. DeMille turned to the Archer with a disdainful smile. "Well, if a little girl like Ciddy can do it, why can't you?"

A few minutes later, hundreds of horsemen and chariot drivers rode down the steep slope, in a cloud of sand.

The dramatic scene concluded as the chariots descended to the bottom of the cliff in clouds of dust. DeMille jumped to his feet. "Cut! That was beautiful. Fantastic."

As the dust cleared, several stunt men writhed and groaned in the sand, covered in blood. Others limped away slowly.

Moments later, the Archer approached DeMille. "Mr. DeMille," he began, "my men are hurting. We need a break."

DeMille pointed to the setting sun. "See that?" he asked.

The Archer winced.

"The Israelites didn't complain about a few bumps and bruises," DeMille continued. "They knew the value of time. Now the sun is setting, we're losing daylight – you got two minutes." He glanced at his watch. "One minute and 55 seconds."

DeMille stood next to the camera, yelling through his megaphone at the charioteers gathered below. "C'mon, you bunch of cowards. Let's make this look real!"

The Archer notched an arrow into his bow and fired it at DeMille's megaphone, the arrow embedding itself into the device just inches from DeMille's head. DeMille looked at arrow sticking out of the megaphone. "Action!"

CHAPTER 27

EXODUS SCENE

DeMille directed a scene where Julia Faye played the part of the pharaoh's wife, Nefretiri. The Exodus proceeded. Completely unrehearsed, the Jewish extras began singing in Hebrew the ancient Hebraic chants, tears streaming down their faces. They sang in unison, "Hear O Israel the Lord Our God, the Lord is One!" and DeMille burst into tears. Ciddy reached for his hand. DeMille smiled at her.

"Truly God is among us," he said.

Later, Egyptians in chariots chased the Israelites across the desert.

Horses stampeded and headed straight for the orchestra, leaving a heap of broken instruments and bruised musicians.

As the dust cleared, Zukor and his assistant Irving arrived on the set. They looked around in amazement. Zukor walked up to DeMille and shook his head. "Well, I didn't know the Israelites played instruments."

Inside DeMille's tent, Zukor waved a stack of papers in his hand. "You're killing me, Cecil! Look at this budget." He waved the stack of papers in front of DeMille.

"We ran into some unexpected situations," DeMille said.

Zukor read items from the budget. "Look. Medical bills - five thousand. Horses - ten thousand. Orchestra equipment - seventeen thousand. What's going on here?"

"We've only got a few more principle scenes to go. Then the second unit can finish up the rest," DeMille replied.

Zukor wasn't putting up with this. "Waive your guaranteed profit," he said, "or cut out the parting of the Red Sea."

DeMille shot scene of Moses in Rameses' throne room, demanding he let his people go. DeMille raised the megaphone. "Cut! Good job people."

DeMille approached Iribe and Marley. "We need to talk about the Red Sea."

CHAPTER 28

PARAMOUNT STUDIOS

DeMille sat in his office, writing in his notebook, when Zukor barged into the room. "I want to preview The Ten Commandments at The Egyptian Theater," said Zukor.

"I've already arranged for a private screening at my home," DeMille replied.

The following night, inside the DeMille home, Paul Berliner conducted the Ritz-Carlton Orchestra in the immense foyer. The elegant African American Woman sang an energetic ragtime number. DeMille, Lasky, Zukor and the other executives squeezed into the study to watch the screening.

HOLLYWOOD, CA 1923

That night the Egyptian Theatre marquee read:

CECIL B. DEMILLE'S

THE TEN COMMANDMENTS
WRITTEN BY JEANIE MACPHERSON

Big stars, reporters, and VIP's gathered for the premiere. DeMille exited a limousine with Constance and Ciddy by his side. Reporters and photographers crowded the scene. Cameras flashed.

Inside the Egyptian Theater, the Red Sea parted in glorious Technicolor®.

CHAPTER 29

HOLLYWOOD GALA

DeMille celebrated the film's success at a big Hollywood gala. He saw his old friend, Sam Goldfish and gave him a big bear hug. "Sam, my old friend! So wonderful to see you, again. It's been a long time."

Lasky joined them. "Gentlemen! Like old times again," he said as though there was never any animosity between him and the others.

"Yes. It certainly is," said DeMille. "Come let's have a drink to celebrate."

A tense moment passed as Goldfish and Lasky eyed each other suspiciously. "Sam. I'm sorry about what happened with Zukor," said Lasky. "I was young and foolish and I hope you can forgive an old fool now."

Goldfish shrugged his shoulders "We have all passed a lot of water since then."

DeMille, Lasky, and Goldfish sat at a large

table. A waiter brought drinks. Goldfish said, "It's like déjà vu all over again. If I could drop dead right now, I'd be the happiest man alive."

The orchestra music rose to a crescendo as the men joked with each other and caught up on old times. DeMille said, "The public is always right, I tell you. And I don't care one hoot about what critics say. I make pictures for people, not for critics."

Goldfish nodded and said, "I say don't pay any attention to the critics. Don't even ignore them."

Lasky looked over at DeMille. "So what's next. C.B.?"

"Something big," said DeMille.

"What could be bigger than the Ten Commandments?" asked Goldfish. "This I gotta see."

CHAPTER 30

DEMILLE OFFICE

DeMille and Jeanie stood in the middle of his office, surrounded by artifacts from The Ten Commandments, including reproductions of the stone tablets perched upon the wall. DeMille handed Jeanie an old, worn Bible and said, "This belonged to my father."

Jeanie took the Bible in her hands reverently. Her hands began to tremble.

"I'm about to give you the most important assignment of your life," he said. "Of my life. Of all our lives."

"Samson and Delilah. Is that it?" she asked.

DeMille placed his hand on Jeanie's shoulder and gazed into the distance. "I will call my next picture The King of Kings."

Jeanie sat down the Bible, lit a cigarette and paced the room. "Another religious picture?" she asked sarcastically. "Zukor's gonna love this."

Two weeks Later, Zukor burst into DeMille's office with the script in his hand. He slammed it down on DeMille's desk. "No more religious pictures," he yelled. "What did I tell you about budget? You're costing Paramount a fortune and I've had enough. That's it."

DeMille stood to his feet and pointed to the door. "Get out," he said.

Zukor glared at DeMille in disbelief. "Nobody tells me to get out. I run this studio. Who do you think you are? Well, I'll tell you. You're nothing. Nothing!"

DeMille came around the desk and grabbed Zukor by the collar, dragging him to the door, slamming him against it. The Ten Commandments Tablets fell from the ledge and broke at Zukor's feet. "I said get the hell out!" shouted DeMille as he threw Zukor out of his office.

Zukor tripped and fell on his face in the hallway. Zukor struggled to his feet, gasping for breath. "That's it," said Zukor. "You're fired, DeMille! And I guarantee you'll never work in this business again. Have your office empty by tomorrow morning."

The next morning DeMille packed his

belongings into cardboard boxes. Two security guards escorted DeMille out of the building.

DeMille stood outside the Paramount Gates, the two cardboard boxes at his feet, when suddenly, he heard a familiar female voice behind him saying, "Not so fast, Mister." He turned around to see Jeanie Macpherson carrying a cardboard box of her own. "Wherever you go, I go," she said.

CHAPTER 31

DEMILLE PICTURES CORPORATION

DeMille stood on the set as members of the clergy offered their blessings. Jesuit priest, Father Daniel A. Lord, led a prayer. "And bless this work, dear Lord, that it may send a message of our Savior's love throughout the world."

DeMille and Jeanie looked at script pages. Researcher Mrs. McGaffey entered with ten packed, typed volumes of notes in her arms. "Here are the research notes," she said as she set the stack of volumes on DeMille's desk.

"Good work, Mrs. McGaffey," said DeMille. "I'll have Jeanie and her staff glean through these over the next couple of weeks."

"I'm on it, C.B." said Jeanie as she started leafing through the volumes.

"Anything urgent that we should be aware

of?" DeMille asked Mrs. McGaffey.

"Well," she began, "according to the Catholic Encyclopedia Volume 4 and Kitto's Encyclopedia Volume 1, the Crown of Thorns was a branch of the bushy Zizyphus Spina Christi, known for its long thorns."

DeMille looked at her impatiently. "Well that's all very interesting, but I don't really see how that…"

Mrs. McGaffey interrupted. "Mr. Wright, the florist obtained two branches from a bush growing on a vacant lot on the corner of Broadway and Sapphire Street in Redondo Beach."

She sparked DeMille's interest. "Ah, so this bush is very rare, you say?"

"Absolutely. I'm not aware of any others in the area," Mrs. McGaffey replied.

DeMille knew he had to act fast. He grabbed Jeanie by the arm. "Jeanie, go down and steal this bush at once."

CHAPTER 32

SCREENING ROOM

DeMille sat in his screening room and watched an old film starring H.B. Warner to make a selection for the leading man.

DeMille walked through the back lot where three thousand extras and fifteen hundred assorted animals and reptiles were gathered. He picked them out one by one, pointing at the chosen ones to stay. Production assistants and animal handlers guided the rejected extras and animals through the back gates.

DeMille oversaw the installation of a ten-stop organ in the studio, to provide inspiration music for the cast. Father Lord approached DeMille and held up a copy of the script. "Mr. DeMille," he began, "I'm afraid that you've taken some unacceptable liberties with the gospel and I must recommend the following changes." He handed DeMille the marked up script. DeMille flipped through the pages, shaking his head and handed the script back to Father Lord.

"Go to hell!" said DeMille to the shocked cleric.

Father Lord was quick with a response. "I'm afraid that won't be possible."

"Oh, is that so?"

Father Lord pointed his finger skyward. "You see, I already have a reservation elsewhere." Father Lord then turned and walked away.

CHAPTER 33

MARY MAGDELENE'S PALACE SET

DeMille assembled a crowd of religious leaders, led by members of every denomination in America, arranging for them to stand in a semi-circle while he addressed them from a pulpit. Several actors, including Joseph Schildkraut (playing Judas Iscariot), and H.B. Warner, (playing the part of Christ) stood in the back of the crowd.

DeMille shouted through his megaphone. "We are on the eve of a very vital thing to the world. So far as I know, it is the first time in history that a group such as this has gathered informally to bless an undertaking. In this little group are represented the great religions of the world, all centered on one point – the life, philosophy, and teachings of a great man."

Rabbis, priests, Hindus wearing turbans,

Buddhist monks, Muslim clerics and protestant ministers nodded their heads in agreement.

DeMille continued. "No matter whether you believe God descended to mortality or mortality rose to Divinity – His life is an open book – no matter what belief, everyone believes this one man has done a great thing for humanity."

DeMille held up his Bible. "We want to give His Work renewed force and vigor and spread it to all parts of the world in order that His motives and sincerity may be understood." DeMille paused and looked around the room slowly, realizing the importance of the moment.

"We have asked representatives of each faith to give us their good thoughts that the right message be given. Thought means so much – hold for us the right thought to help us do our bit toward spreading the great gospel that this great man taught."

The crowd erupted in applause, assuming DeMille was done with his speech. But DeMille continued, "As we gather on this momentous occasion, I'd like to say a few words about the meaning of the New Testament." Several of the men in the crowd begin looking at each other, shifting positions and glancing at their pocket watches.

SIX HOURS LATER

"Now we come to the Gospel according to Luke where I will provide you all with an explanation of the geneologies and how they differ from the lineage described in the Matthew's Gospel. In fact, why don't we return to the book of Matthew for a few minutes as a refresher?" By now the men were all looking exhausted, looking at their watches, shifting positions, leaning against each other for support.

Suddenly a faint unintelligible cry echoed from the back of the room.

DeMille looked up. "Who was that?" he asked as he looked around the room.

A faint voice echoed from the back of the room. "It is I!" Judas appeared at the back of the crowd. "Can't I let Jesus sit down? I've been propping him up for the past two hours."

Judas held up Jesus (played by H.B. Warner) with his arm around his shoulders, keeping him from falling.

CHAPTER 34

DEMILLE OFFICE

Actress Dorothy Cummings, beautiful with dark flowing hair played the part of the Virgin Mary. She sat before DeMille at his desk reading the contract. She looked up at DeMille with a frown. "I see here where it says that I should bind myself absolutely to you to regulate my personal life that no possible blemish of character may eventuate."

DeMille nodded. "That, my dear, simply means that you are not to attract scandal, not even to divorce your husband during the filming and initial run of the film."

"I see," said Cummings. She picked up a pen and signed her name at the bottom.

The radio announcer's voice filtered through the air. "Verily there was light and a thousand 'extras' did flock to the scene as a thousand moths eager to singe their wings upon the flames of the Klieg lamps. And there arose before them the graven images of DeMille and they bowed down their heads to him and there was heard in Hollywood a terrible din."

DeMille met with a young immigrant woman. Her head was wrapped in a scarf. "So you're new to America," DeMille began. "That's great. Just think your first job will be one of great importance. Not everyone can say they worked as an extra in a DeMille film."

The woman spoke with a heavy Russian accent. "Thank you so much, Mr. DeMille. I promise to work very hard for you. I promised my mother that I would come to America and make something of myself."

"You're in the land of opportunity, my dear. You can do anything you dream of doing. The sky's the limit. Who knows, you may become a famous actress."

The Immigrant Woman laughed shyly, covering her mouth and shaking her head. "Oh, no sir. That's not for me. I want to be a writer. A great writer."

"Writing is a very noble profession," said DeMille. "I hope you do well."

The Woman stood to leave. Turning to DeMille again she said, "Thank you again, Mr.

DeMille. For giving me a new start here in America." The woman turned and walks toward the door.

"Oh, I'm sorry, Miss. Tell me your name?"

The woman stopped and turned. "I am called Ayn. Ayn Rand."

Her accent was so thick that DeMille could barely understand what she said. "Good luck to you, Anne," he said.

"Not Anne. My name is Ayn. Sounds like wine."

A handsome actor named Frank Conner, 20s, handsome passed by. DeMille called out to him. "Oh, Frank. Could you come here a moment?"

"Anne. This is Frank Conner, he'll show you to the women's quarters."

Frank led the Immigrant Woman away. Ayn turned to him and said, "I am called Ayn."

"Oh, like wine," he said. "I like that." Little did anyone know at that moment that Frank Conner and Ayn Rand would soon be married and that Ayn would go on to write several bestselling novels, including *Atlas Shrugged* and *The Fountainhead*.

CHAPTER 35

STUDIO BACK LOT

DeMille walked through the back lot of his studio where he witnessed a handler training one hundred white doves to fly across the stage in formation. In another section, he saw Mary Magdalene's leopard pace about a golden cage. A brilliantly plumaged Bird of Paradise sunned itself behind a wire netting under a giant arc light.

DeMille oversaw the shipping of seventy-five tons of props in fifteen trucks to the docks at San Pedro, where an entire passenger steamer waited to take cast, staff, and props across the water.

DeMille directed scenes by the Sea of Galilee filmed in Catalina and later, a scene with Julia as Martha at the tomb of Lazarus. He wept as he directed the scene of Jesus forgiving Mary Magdalene.

DeMille filmed a tremendous earthquake where dust swirled high by fierce winds.

Rabbi Magnin stood in front of DeMille at his desk. DeMille rose to greet him. "On behalf of B'Nai B'Rith organization, I congratulate you for doing such a fine work about a man of peace. God bless you, Mr. DeMille."

DeMille and Rabbi Magnin shook hands.

A Muslim Imam bowed with folded hands in front of DeMille, who returned the gesture. "Jesus is a central figure in our religion as well," said the Imam. "I pray that this work will bring people of all faiths together in peace and brotherhood."

"Thank you sir," said DeMille. That is my hope as well."

Later, DeMille sat as his desk as the radio announcer's voice filtered through the air. "Several British cities, including London, have banned Cecil B. DeMille's epic film portrayal of Jesus in The King of Kings due to special ordinances prohibiting the public display of Christ's face."

Searchlights arced across the night sky. Hundreds of fans, reporters and celebrities crowded into the historic Grauman's Chinese Theater, which opened with the premiere of *King of Kings*, and the film enjoyed wide public acclaim.

Rabbi Magnin stood next to DeMille as reporters and photographers gathered. He raised his voice so the crowd could hear him. "A great story is bound about a great man to bring about love and peace. Yet the One who has preached love and peace has been the center of such controversy that streams of blood have flowed to the sea. This story, free from any theology, will bring home to the world the true message that the great teacher taught through visual education."

CHAPTER 36

SCREENING ROOM

DeMille sat alone in the screening room watching King of Kings, sobbing at the scene of Mary Magdalene wiping the feet of Christ with her hair. He held his pistol in his lap.

BANG!

Constance looked down at the iron skillet on the kitchen floor. DeMille rushed in. "Honey, are you okay?"

Constance reached down and picked up the skillet. "Oh, I'm sorry dear. I don't even remember why I needed that skillet. Supper is almost ready."

"You look tired, come sit," said DeMille.

Constance looked bewildered. "What?"

DeMille gestured her to sit down. Constance stared at his face as if she was seeing him for the first time.

"What?" DeMille asked.

"When did you get wrinkles?" Constance asked. Her voice was sad.

Later, DeMille and Constance sat at the dinner table together. They stared fondly at each other through the glowing candles.

"Connie, can you possibly find it in your heart to forgive my transgressions?" DeMille asked.

Constance smiled at him warmly, reaching across the table and putting her hand on his. "What transgressions? I don't even remember what they were." She rose from the table and heads towards the stairs. She stopped and turned to DeMille. "Aren't you coming up to bed?" she asked. She turned and headed up the stairs.

DeMille jumped up and followed her to the bedroom. Constance opened the bedroom door and beckoned DeMille to follow her inside. DeMille entered the bedroom, closing the door behind him.

CHAPTER 37

OCTOBER 29, 1929

At the New York stock exchange, men panicked as they watched the numbers on the board tumble. Shots of newspaper headlines screamed about the Great Depression. Men stood in soup lines. Others jumped out of skyscraper windows.

Zukor sat at his desk smoking a cigar. DeMille stood before him, hat in hand. "Times have been tough for everybody, Cecil," Zukor said. "Business is bad."

DeMille put his hat back on his head. "You asked me to come down here to tell me that? You're the one who fired me, remember? I don't know what I was thinking." DeMille turned and headed toward the door.

Zukor stood to his feet and called out to DeMille. "Wait. I need your help."

DeMille exited Zukor's office and headed

down the long hallway.

Zukor followed him. "Paramount needs your help!"

DeMille kept walking, not looking back.

Zukor shouted to DeMille. "You'll have total creative control!"

CHAPTER 38

CLEOPATRA SET

In Cleopatra's elegant palace, Henry Wilcoxen, as Marc Antony stood in front of an empty throne. The gorgeous Claudette Colbert, as Cleopatra, dressed in all her regalia, entered and takes her seat on the throne. DeMille stood behind the camera with his megaphone. The camera moved in for a close up on Cleopatra.

"I am Cleopatra," she said. "Queen of the Nile!"

Ciddy stepped up next to DeMille. She looked at him and smiled adoringly. Jeanie stood in the wings smoking a cigarette, coughing loudly.

1948

On the set of *Samson and Delilah* an elderly Jeanie, collapsed in exhaustion. DeMille ran to her side. "Jeanie! Somebody call a doctor!"

A doctor arrived and gave Jeanie a quick check up with his stethoscope. "I think she needs to come in for some tests," he said.

Jeanie slowly rose to her feet and lit a cigarette. "Don't worry about me," she said. "I'm fine. Just a little tired. That's all."

DeMille put his arm around her. "I think you should listen to the doctor," he said.

Jeanie shook her head. "I just need some rest." She said. "If it's okay, can I just take the rest of the day off? Just tired. So...very tired."

DeMille helped Jeanie to a waiting limo.

DeMille sat at his desk writing as the voice of the radio announcer droned in the background. DeMille stopped when he heard the announcer say, "Silent screen legend, Norma Desmond was arrested tonight at her Hollywood mansion for the murder of young screenwriter, Joe Gillis."

Earlier that night, police had led Norma out of the mansion in handcuffs as screenwriter Joe Gillis floated face down in her swimming pool. Photographers surrounded the place, flashing their cameras.

DeMille sat in his office, writing in his

notebook. Jeanie approached DeMille, looking tired and gaunt. DeMille stood up and moved from behind his desk to greet her. "Jeanie. Please sit down." He guided her to the couch. "May I get you something? Some water?"

"Water would be nice," she said.

DeMille poured Jeanie a glass of water and handed it to her. He sat on the couch next to her.

Jeanie took a sip of the water and set it down on the table. She laid her head on DeMille's shoulder and began sobbing uncontrollably. DeMille comforted her. "There, there," he said. "It's alright." He stroked her hair.

"No, C.B. It's not alright." She wept. "The doc says it's cancer."

DeMille lowered his head. "Dear God," he whispered. "Is there anything I can do to help? Do you need money?"

Jeanie shook her head as she struggled to her feet. DeMille helped her up. Jeanie walked away. She stopped and turned toward DeMille. She looked at him with longing and remembrance. "Forget about me, C.B. Go take care of your wife." She walked out of the office.

DeMille followed her. "Jeanie," he implored. "Wait...Please."

Jeanie turned to him and said, "Go take care of your wife." She gave DeMille a friendly salute, turned, and walked away. Not looking back, she stopped, lit a cigarette and began coughing uncontrollably.

Jeanie laid in the hospital bed, pale and thin, eyes closed. DeMille entered with a single red rose in hand. "Jeanie," he whispered. "Can you hear me?"

Jeanie lay still. DeMille approached the bed and touched Jeanie's cheek. "You were right --- if I had let you walk out the door, I would have regretted it… for the rest of my life. You were absolutely worth ten times that amount." DeMille turned and left the room, red rose still in hand.

DeMille stood alone in front of Jeanie's headstone and gently laid the red rose on her grave. He walked home alone.

CHAPTER 39

Inside the Ambassador Hotel, a banner across the ballroom read:

HAPPY 50TH ANNIVERSARY.

The 32-piece Ritz-Carlton orchestra played fast and joyous music as well dressed guests glided across the dance floor. DeMille and Constance sat at the head table. Friends and family celebrated around them. DeMille motioned with his hand and the waiter brought over a large box, placing it down in front of Constance. He looked at her adoringly. "Well, open it," he said.

Constance sat there apparently overcome with emotion.

DeMille opened the box, revealing a solid

gold dinner set. Constance clapped her hands in delight. "Oh, it's lovely!" she exclaimed.

DeMille motioned and the waiter brought over another, smaller box. DeMille opened it in front of Constance, revealing the old silver set from the pawnshop. "Just a little something to remind you of old times. We've come a long way, haven't we?"

Constance clasped her hands in front of her. She looked at DeMille with a dazed, puzzled look. "What did you say your name was?"

The music suddenly stopped playing as Constance stared blankly into space.

Inside their bedroom that evening, Constance stared blankly as she rocked in a chair. DeMille, holding a Bible, helplessly watched. Ciddy placed her hand on his shoulder. DeMille kissed Ciddy's hand. "I'm being punished you know," he said.

"Father."

"All these years I've been trying to prove something to my Dad. Show him that I was worthy of him. Somewhere along the line, I missed the truly big picture... It's not about the extras, the lighting, the spectacular..." He smiled. "It's ironic.... The true magic of one's vision is not captured in a canister..."

Ciddy listened.

He choked up and touched his heart. "It's captured in your soul."

CHAPTER 40

PARAMOUNT STUDIOS

Zukor sat alone in the screening room and watched the scene from the 1923 version of *The Ten Commandments*, where Moses descended from Mt. Sinai with the stone tablets.

Later that evening, Zukor sat at his desk with an open Bible in front of him.

Inside DeMille's office, an elderly Julia Faye sat across from DeMille. Julia spoke softly. "I have a big confession to make, sugar."

DeMille interrupted. "I've saved a part for you."

"You mean you've forgiven me after all these years?" she asked.

"I've been forgiven much. How could I not forgive you, Julia? But let's not talk about that anymore. What is done is done."

"Momma told me never to lie, but I lied to you," she said.

"What's that?"

"I lied about the whole thing."

"What in heaven are you talking about?"

Julia hung her head and sighed. "I just wanted you to love me."

"Julia, I'm sorry but none of this is making any sense. Let's just forget about the past and move on." He stood up and started toward the door, motioning for Julia to follow.

"Don't you hear what I'm saying? I made the whole thing up. I was never pregnant. There was no abortion. It was all lies. Lies. Lies!" Julia broke down sobbing as DeMille held her in his arms. "Oh, Julia. Julia. Julia."

"Do you still forgive me?" she asked.

CHAPTER 41

ZUKOR'S OFFICE

DeMille stood at Zukor's desk. Zukor, with his back to DeMille sat looking out the window. DeMille put his hands on his hips. "We're shooting in Egypt this time."

Zukor turned around in his chair. He was old and serene. Zukor picked up his phone. "Give Mr. DeMille carte blanche. Anything he wants." He paused for a moment. "That's right." Zukor hung up the phone, smiled gently at DeMille, nodded and lifted his hand in consent.

Inside the screening room that night, DeMille watched the scene from the 1923 *Ten Commandments* where Pharaoh agreed to let Moses and his people go.

CHAPTER 42

PARAMOUNT STUDIOS

DeMille dug through old files. He took out copies of Jeanie's old *Ten Commandments* scripts and development notes.

DeMille and crew arrived at the Port of Alexandria in Egypt by ship with hundreds of animals and tons of equipment.

Actor Edward G. Robinson, 60's stood in front of DeMille dressed in Egyptian robes for the role of Dathan. "I thought I'd never work again," said Robinson. "But you took a chance and gave me break. I'll never forget you." Robinson wept as DeMille gave him a big bear hug, slapping him on the back.

"Let's pray those days are behind us," said DeMille.

CHAPTER 43

EGYPTIAN PALACE

DeMille, Ciddy, Henry Wilcoxen, and starring actor Charlton Heston arrived at the palace of Egyptian President Naguib, who was heavy set and dressed in a tuxedo. A servant led DeMille and his group into the front room, where Naguib was seated. Naguib stood and greeted DeMille. "Mr. DeMille. I greet you and your guests on this wonderful occasion. Let me assure you of your complete safety and welfare as long as you are in Egypt."

DeMille, Ciddy, Wilcoxen, and Heston took their seats at the elegant dinner table.

Suddenly, Egyptian soldiers stormed the palace with machine guns pointed in every direction.

Ciddy leaned over to DeMille's protective arms. "Father! What's happening? Dear God, they're going to kills us all!"

DeMille whispered to Ciddy. "Don't worry honey. They wouldn't dare hurt us. We're Americans."

Heston stood to his feet and reached for the pistol in his waistband. "What's the meaning of this?" Heston demanded.

An Egyptian solder pointed a machine gun at Heston's head and shook his head. Heston took his hand away from his gun and raised his hands above his head.

One of Naguib's guards pulled out a gun and the Egyptian soldier shot him dead.

Ciddy screamed.

The Egyptian Soldier subdued President Naguib and his men, forcing them to their knees with hands above their heads. Soldiers led President Naguib away in handcuffs. Prime Minister Gamel Abdel-Nasser, wearing a military uniform, entered the palace, flanked by two armed soldiers.

Nasser turned to DeMille and smiled. "Do not worry, Mr. DeMille. Now that I am in charge, let me assure you of your complete safety and welfare as long as you are in Egypt."

CHAPTER 44

MT. SINAI

DeMille arrived at the foot of Mt. Sinai with a fleet of cars, cameras, cast and crew. He met with the monks at the Monastery of St. Catherine. A poor Bedouin woman greeted them. "We don't have much," she said. "But all we have is yours."

Egyptian desert, pyramids, the Great Sphinx loomed in the background. DeMille directed the scene where Ziphora, a beautiful Bedouin woman humbly greeted Moses with hospitality. "We don't have much," she said. "But all we have is yours."

DeMille was on the set, about to film the next scene. He stood in front of a huge crowd of extras. "OK, people. Let's try this scene again. Marley, get another shot of the Sphinx. Then push in for a close up of Heston." He looked around. "Now I want you extras to spread out a little. I need people here, here, and here." DeMille points to various locations on the set when he suddenly noticed Female Extra #1 talking to another female extra. He approached her. "Will you kindly tell everyone here what you are talking about and what is so important?"

Female Extra #1 replied, "I was just saying to my friend, "I wonder when that bald-headed son of a bitch is going to call lunch."

DeMille glared at the extra for a moment, then broke into a broad smile and yelled. "Lunch!"

The wind swept sparkling desert sands against the steep cliffs. DeMille, dressed in his signature high boots, jodhpurs, and carrying a big megaphone sat in his director's chair. Standing next to DeMille was Ciddy, naturally pretty; her kind eyes shimmered with the natural wonder and imagination of a young girl. DeMille handed Ciddy his wooden cane, worn by time and use. "Can you keep an eye on this?" he asked.

Ciddy took the cane in her hands and looked at it fondly. "Oh, you think you don't need it anymore?"

"Something like that," he said.

A camera assistant claps the slate. "The Ten Commandments. Scene 70."

DeMille raised the megaphone to his mouth. "Action!"

Hundreds of horses and chariots headed down the edge of the cliffs and down their steep incline. Three cameramen caught the action from different angles. The chariots descended to the bottom of the steep dunes in clouds of dust.

DeMille stood to his feet. "Cut! That was fantastic. Perfect."

Moments later, DeMille looked over to Cameraman #1, raising the megaphone again. "Did you get that?"

Cameraman #1 pointed to what's left of his camera, half buried in the sand. "Sorry, C.B. The camera got trampled in the stampede."

DeMille looked to Cameraman #2. The cameraman looked at the front of the camera and wiped a big clod of dirt from the lens. He looked back at DeMille and shook his head.

DeMille jumped up and ran around frantically waving his arms at everybody, looking up to heaven, desperately pleading with God to save this precious shot. He lifted up his megaphone toward Cameraman #3. "Please tell me your camera is working."

Cameraman #3 nodded, smiled and gave DeMille a thumbs up. "Ready when you are, C.B."

CHAPTER 45

TEN COMMANDMENTS SET

DeMille climbed with producer Henry Wilcoxen to the top of one of the one-hundred-foot gates, up an almost perpendicular ladder. As DeMille reached the top, he staggered and fell to his knees, unable to breathe. Wilcoxen came to his aid and reached out his hand. "Let me help you, Chief."

DeMille impatiently brushed him aside. Out of breath. "I'm okay. I can do this."

DeMille slowly reached the ground, and then sank to a sitting position on the ground. Ciddy ran to DeMille and helped him make his way to his director's chair. "Father! Are you alright?"

Wilcoxen brought DeMille a glass of water. DeMille's eyes rolled back in his head and he passed out in the chair. Wilcoxen yelled, "Somebody get the doc over here. Now!"

The doctor ran to DeMille and checked his

heart with a stethoscope. DeMille opened his eyes and pushed the stethoscope away. "What's all this fuss? I'm perfectly fine."

"I'm going to need you to sit still and rest for awhile," the doctor said.

Ciddy kneeled at DeMille's side. "Father. Tell me what you want to do."

DeMille smiled at her fondly. "Make sure the final act is right."

CHAPTER 46

EGYPTIAN HIGHWAY

Ciddy drove DeMille down the highway. "You don't have to worry. I'll take care of everything," she said.

DeMille coughed and struggled to catch his breath. "Thanks, dear. I just need to rest tonight."

Ciddy returned to the set alone and picked up DeMille's megaphone, holding it by her side while cast and crew members stood around restlessly. "OK, people. Let's get back to work."

Nobody responded to Ciddy's orders. She lifted the megaphone to her mouth. "Let's go! Places everybody! We've got a picture to make!" Everyone scurried to proper positions.

Inside DeMille's apartment that night, DeMille laid quietly in his bed, barely awake.

Ciddy sat by his side. The doctor entered the room. "I'm afraid I've got some bad news, Mr. DeMille," he said. "It's your heart. You can't take anymore stress right now. I must tell you to abandon the direction of the picture."

"You can't make him stop now," Ciddy said. "This is his life."

"He could die if he continues working," the doctor replied.

"He'll die if he stops working!"

DeMille stretched out his hand. "I cannot quit now. This is God's work. I must not fail Him."

That night DeMille got down on his knees beside the bed and prayed fervently.

The red sun rose over the sweeping Egyptian desert, illuminating the set with dances of light and shadow. The dawn broke through DeMille's bedroom window. He rose from his bed and lifted his hands toward heaven. "Do I hear applause?" He took a deep breath and let it out in a slow sigh.

The cast and crew applauded DeMille's return to the set. He walked feebly with a cane and took his seat in his director's chair.

DeMille directed Julia in a one-line scene as an old woman in the Passover scene. Julia sat huddled at the table with the other Israelites as the Angel of Death approached. "Will it pass?" she asked. "Will it pass?"

DeMille lifted the megaphone to his mouth. "Cut! Good job everyone."

The cast and crew applauded as DeMille rose from his director's chair.

DeMille celebrated with cast and crew. Everybody danced and sang to traditional Middle Eastern music.

At the Egyptian Theater in Hollywood, the crowd buzzed with anticipation of what they were about to witness.

In the filmed introduction, DeMille stood on the stage before the movie began. "The theme of this picture is whether men are to be ruled by God's law or whether they are to be ruled by the whims of a dictator like Rameses," DeMille began. "Are men the property of the state or are they free souls under God? This same battle continues throughout the world today."

DeMille left the premiere with Ciddy. A man

stood across the street with his hand in his jacket pocket, watching DeMille.

The man looked around cautiously and crossed the street. He approached DeMille with his hand still in his jacket pocket.

"Mr. Cecil B. DeMille?" the man asked.

"Why yes, DeMille answered. "Do I know you?"

The man pulled his hand from his jacket pocket revealing a court summons.

Reporters and photographers gathered. Cameras flashed.

CHAPTER 47

COURTROOM

Judge Ray Morton, glasses perched on his nose, sat behind the bench. The bailiff called the court to order. "Oyez. Oyez. Oyez. The Superior Court of California in the District of Los Angeles shall now come to order. Honorable Judge Ray Morton presiding. Case of Suratt vs. DeMille before the court, wherein the plaintiff is suing the defendant for the amount of one million dollars."

Members of the audience gasped and murmured.

The judge slammed the gavel. He looked over his glasses at the files in front of him. "Order in my courtroom. Order, I say! This is a court of law not a circus."

DeMille sat at the defendant's table with his attorney. Ciddy, Goldfish and Lasky sat in the gallery.

Mrs. Surratt was in her 40s and wore excessive make up like an old screen vamp. She sat with her attorney at the plaintiff's table.

Mrs. Suratt took the stand first. "I wrote this story ten years ago," she began, "and submitted it to Mr. DeMille over at Paramount Studios. I was told that he would let me know if he was interested and if so, I would be justly compensated. I want a million dollars."

DeMille took the stand. He said, "I have always been under the impression that Moses was the first to write the story of the Exodus. If Mrs. Suratt was its original author and predates him, then the record will have to be changed."

The courtroom erupted in laughter and the judge banged his gavel. "Order! Order!"

The courtroom quieted down. The judge cleared his throat. "You may step down Mr. DeMille."

DeMille returned to his seat. "Thank you your honor."

"In light of the facts of this case, it appears that Mrs. Suratt has not provided any compelling evidence that neither she nor her written work precede that of Moses and the book of Exodus. Therefore, I am dismissing this case."

The courtroom exploded in applause and

DeMille stood up to leave. The judge banged his gavel again. "Not so fast, Mr. DeMille. I still have one final question before I adjourn this procedure."

"Yes, your honor?"

"How did you pull off the crossing of the Red Sea?"

DeMille passed a stone plaque of the Ten Commandments as he exited the courthouse. He stood next to it as photographers took his picture. FLASH.

CHAPTER 48

THE BROWN DERBY

Glamorous celebrities and wannabe starlets mingled at the trendy Brown Derby restaurant on Wilshire Boulevard, all trying to look their best. DeMille, Lasky, and Goldfish, now all up in age, met again and reminisced.

DeMille basked in his success, pouring forth the wisdom of the ages. "The way I see it," he began, "a picture is made a success not on a set but over the drawing board. Once you come out with a great script, you got a great picture."

Lasky and Goldfish nodded in agreement.

DeMille continued. "I don't go in for all that on the set revision stuff. These new directors are crazy. And the trash they're making."

Goldfish smirked. "I just hired a new director. We're overpaying him, but he's worth it. I told him to spare no expense to save money on my next picture."

The waiter brought drinks.

Lasky never quite got over the guilt he felt from his lack of loyalty. He had seen many good times, but this was not among them. "Sam here has done very well for himself. I say it's a lot of luck," he said, pointing to Goldfish with passive-aggressive envy.

"I say, the harder I work, the luckier I get," said Sam. He looked at the two smugly. "So tell me, C.B., how did you love my movies?"

"I absolutely loved *The Best Years of Our Lives* and congratulations again on your Oscar."

Goldfish beamed with pride. "And my comedies aren't something to laugh at either."

DeMille chuckled and took a drink. "And you did a marvelous job with *Guys and Dolls*. You've done great work, Sam Goldfish. Keep it up."

Goldfish interjected. "Oh, by the way. It's no longer Sam Goldfish. The last name is Goldwyn now."

"Goldwyn?" DeMille asked.

"I went into business with Max Selwyn, so we decided to make a company with both of our names combined. Goldfish and Selwyn. And Selfish didn't sound so good, so we went with Goldwyn. I decided I liked the name and kept it for myself as part of the deal."

DeMille laughed and shook his head. Goldwyn took a drink and continued. "The sad truth of the matter is that it's hard for us Jews to get anywhere in this movie business. I mean who's going to hire a guy by the name of Goldfish? So I do what I can to get by." Goldwyn shrugged his shoulders.

Lasky lit a cigarette. "If I didn't need the money I'd get out of this business," he said. "But I've agreed to go back to Paramount for one more picture. It's so funny. I feel like I'm losing it sometimes. I'm even thinking about seeing a psychiatrist."

Goldwyn shook his head and laughed. "Anybody who goes to a psychiatrist ought to have his head examined."

Lasky stood up to leave. He took a drag from his cigarette, and then lifted his glass. "L'Chaim," he toasted.

DeMille and Lasky lifted their glasses to Lasky and toasted in unison, "L'Chaim".

Lasky downed the rest of his drink, and then dropped his glass on the floor, where it shattered. He grabbed his heart and then fell over face down on the table.

DeMille and Goldwyn carried the casket at Lasky's funeral.

CHAPTER 49

1959 HOLLYWOOD

DeMille walked through Paramount Studio with his cane, smiling and waving at the multitude of stars, executives, and studio employees. He entered his office sat down at his old familiar desk.

For the rest of the day, DeMille handed out checks to members of the cast and crew, as they entered his office, paying homage and giving thanks, one by one.

Inside the DeMille home that night, DeMille, frail and in poor health, laid in his bed writing in his red notebook. Ciddy and her husband Joseph Harper came to visit, bringing along their beautiful five-year-old daughter Cecilia.

"Father, you've fought the good fight. That's more than anyone can ask. Why don't you rest now for awhile and let me take care of you."

"I need to put my affairs in order," he said.

Adolph Zukor entered the room, hat in hand and approached DeMille's bedside. Zukor gripped DeMille's hand and the two men remained silent for a long moment.

Zukor finally let go of DeMille's grip and wiped a tear from his eye. He spoke softly. "So tell me all about your next project, C.B. What do you want to do?"

DeMille looked up with a twinkle in his eyes. "Another picture, I imagine, or, perhaps, another world."

Later that evening, DeMille began to scribble in his notebook, part prayer, part obituary. "The Lord giveth and the Lord taketh away. Blessed be the name of the Lord. It can only be a short time..." DeMille stopped writing for a moment and looked upward. He took a deep breath and continued. "...until those words, the first in the Episcopal funeral services are spoken over me. . . After those words are spoken, what am I? I am only what I have accomplished. How much good have I spread? How much evil have I spread? For whatever I am a moment after death--a spirit, a soul, a bodiless mind--I shall have to look back and forward, for I have to take with me both."

The morning sun shined softly in DeMille's

bedroom. DeMille had a fatal heart attack and took his final breath with Ciddy by his side. Constance, who had become lost in senile dementia and no longer recognized DeMille, sat in a rocking chair, staring blankly into space, oblivious.

The red notebook fell to the floor beside DeMille's bed.

Adolph Zukor, Sam Goldwyn, and Henry Wilcoxen helped carry DeMille's casket. Ciddy stood beside her mother, Constance who stared into the distance, smiling. Ciddy's daughter, Cecilia, held the red notebook in her hands.

Reverend Lord gave the eulogy. "The Lord giveth. The Lord taketh away. Blessed be the name of the Lord."

The radio announcer's voice filtered in the distance. "The world mourns the passing of legendary director Cecil B. DeMille. According to a New York Times op-ed piece this morning, 'Mr. DeMille combined the flair for showmanship of a Barnum with the cinematic inventiveness of a Griffith.'"

The service concluded and the participants dispersed. The radio announcer continued his salute. "Cecil B. DeMille will certainly be missed but not forgotten."

The cemetery was empty. A single red rose lay beneath the headstone, which simply read,

CECIL B. DEMILLE
1881 – 1959

A woman wearing a red dress stood in the distance beside a tree.

EPILOGUE

And he said unto me,
"Behold the new land
with thine eyes, for thou shalt not cross over this
River Jordan."

OLD THEATER

The red butterfly fluttered into the window of the dark and empty theater, touching down only for a holy instant on the empty stage, then off again, up and out the window vanishing into the sun.

Inside the theater, the faded curtains hung loosely, worn by time and inattention as an unseen man's voice shouted, "Action!" The single word echoed, multiplying through the lonely timbers, resonating in the air, and then fading into nothingness.

Nothing happened. The long silence begged for interruption.

"I said action!" The man's voice grew louder, stronger, echoing once again across the empty stage.

"Where the hell is everyone?" His voice betrayed a desperate tone. A shaft of sunlight angled in through the window, revealing the signature custom boots of aging, balding Cecil B. DeMille. He wore jodhpurs and carried a large megaphone. He rose from his Director's chair. "Where are my extras?"

Nothing, but an empty stage.

Then a hand drew back the stage curtain. DeMille frowned, his vision hazy as if he was looking through a veil. Through the veil, he saw an attractive woman dressed in red holding a rose. She beckoned him to come to her. He hesitated. From behind the curtain, she stretched forth her hand and motioned for him to come. DeMille slowly climbed the stairs to the stage. He looked back at his empty Director's chair. Then back to her. She smiled. He shuffled forward toward the curtain. She stepped back and gestured him in. He looked back once more at his empty Director's chair. Then he looked forward.

Suddenly a smile broke out on his face. He raised his megaphone and directed – "No! No! More lighting. I need more lighting!" He stepped into the curtain. The curtain closed behind him. The empty Director's chair remained emblazoned with the name Cecil B. DeMille.

About the author

ROBERT HAMMOND is an award-winning screenwriter, producer and author of over 10 books, including *Ready When You Are: Cecil B. DeMille's Ten Commandments for Success*. He holds an MFA in Creative Writing and is a highly sought-after speaker on personal achievement, filmmaking and Hollywood history. His film projects include the documentary *One Day on Earth* and epic biopic *C.B. DeMille*.

Credits

SPECIAL THANKS TO:
Lesa Hammond
Gabrielle Evans-Fields
Brandon Pender
Frank Montesonti
Helen Kantor
Ariane Simard
Ken Burke
Fay Guilian
Tynya Beverly
Rob Gallagher
Terri Zinner
Daniel Gebretensai
Michael Beazel
Kurt St. Angelo
AJ Williams
Jim Wilkington
Ryan Gilmore
Los Angeles New Wave International Film
Hollywood Heritage Foundation

READY WHEN YOU ARE:
CECIL B. DEMILLE'S TEN COMMANDMENTS FOR SUCCESS

What if the visionary director who invented Hollywood and the Biblical epic offered you his personal secrets to unlimited wealth and achievement?

Ready When You Are: Cecil B. DeMille's Ten Commandments for Success (New Way Press) weaves the timeless wisdom of one of the greatest showman on earth into a detailed roadmap for successful living today.

In his latest book, comparable to such classics as *The 7 Habits of Highly-Effective People, Think and Grow Rich,* and *Leadership Secrets of Attila the Hun,* author Robert Hammond reveals C.B. DeMille's secret strategies to achieve a life of career success and personal fulfillment. In addition to being an inspirational self-help book, *Ready When You Are* also includes scholarly research on the influence of Cecil B. DeMille's Biblical epics as well as recently-discovered articles on filmmaking written by DeMille himself.